JUN - - 2022

Goddess Girls

PERSEPHONE
THE
DARING

Goddess Girls

PERSEPHONE
THE DARING

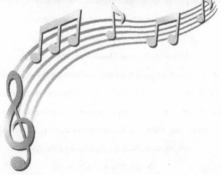

JOAN HOLUB & SUZANNE WILLIAMS

Aladdin

NEW YORK   LONDON   TORONTO   SYDNEY   NEW DELHI

ALADDIN

An imprint of Simon & Schuster Children's Publishing Division

1230 Avenue of the Americas, New York, NY 10020

First Aladdin hardcover edition August 2013

Copyright © 2013 by Joan Holub and Suzanne Williams

All rights reserved, including the right of reproduction in whole or in part in any form.

ALADDIN is a trademark of Simon & Schuster, Inc., and related logo is a registered trademark
of Simon & Schuster, Inc.

Also available in an Aladdin paperback edition.

For information about special discounts for bulk purchases, please contact
Simon & Schuster Special Sales at 1-866-506-1949 or business@simonandschuster.com.

The Simon & Schuster Speakers Bureau can bring authors to your live event. For more information or
to book an event contact the Simon & Schuster Speakers Bureau at 1-866-248-3049
or visit our website at www.simonspeakers.com.

Designed by Karin Paprocki

The text of this book was set in Baskerville Handcut Regular.

Manufactured in the United States of America 0417 QVE

2 4 6 8 10 9 7 5 3

Library of Congress Control Number 2013931642

ISBN 978-1-4424-8158-9 (hc)

ISBN 978-1-4424-4939-8 (pbk)

ISBN 978-1-4424-4940-4 (eBook)

We appreciate our mega-amazing readers!
Catherine O., Meyrick M., Sabrina E., Sophia E.,
Rashmi L., Shannon G., Mona P., Lex C., Jenny C.,
Breanna J., Victoria R., Zoya B., Katya B., Annie C.,
Juliette M., Madison T., Chloe M., Ryanna L., Sierra G.,
Evilynn R., Jaylee T., Olivia M., Abby G., Pam L., Audra J.,
Scout L., Grace D., Kristen S., Mariane D., Monica K.,
Sydney S., Tina L., Justine Y., Sofia W., Lily T., Elaine M.,
Serena G., Cynthia Y., Rayana W., Charisma L., Izzy F.,
Izabel K., Prisca M., Mariah M., Jadalynn F., Olivia R.,
Stephanie S., Keana H., Amanda W., Kierra C., Kristin B.,
Jasmine L., Emily M., Cala I., Justess I., Kevin M., Joe P.,
Ella S., Sydney G., Lily P., Ally W., Kari W., Helena L.,
the Andrade family, Ericka A., Joy M., Jessica N., Corey H.,
Chelsea G., Medusa D., Ray J. M., Amaya M., Jada C.,
Alba C., Ashlyn L., Carolyn D., Stephanie T., Emma J.,
Lucie N., Sarah S., Olivia B., Aaliyah H., Abbie M.,
Michey J., Ecenur U., Sara S., Ryan M., Amber A., Karis C.,
Rowan W., Savannah R., Gaby G., Monet's Mom, Dana P.,
Sydney B., Ashley C., Kelsey H., Shaelie M., Malerie G.,
Sabrina L., Leah M., Jocelyn D., Kennedy D., Sierra A.,
Denise D., Avery T., Sydney T., Sabrina P., Liza B., Natalie S.,
Kaya P., Lara P., Leah H., Meghan B., Natasha H.,
Juliah D., Anna P., Victoria B., Jessica S., Lana W.,
Julia T., Rebecca K., and you!

–J. H. and S. W.

CONTENTS

1

Gym Sleepover

Persephone

PERSEPHONE'S ARMS WERE LOADED WITH HER overnight stuff as she walked into the school gym Friday night. Looking around, she saw that the gym floor was covered with a big jumble of sleeping bags, snacks, makeup, board games, and a few stuffed animals. A huge glittery sign on the far wall read: MOUNT OLYMPUS ACADEMY GIRLS' ATHLETICS SLEEPOVER TONIGHT!

Most of the girls were already here by now. It had taken Persephone longer to arrive because she was one of the few MOA students who didn't live in the Academy dorm. Instead she lived with her mom, Demeter, on Earth. And she'd forgotten to bring her overnight things from home this morning. So she'd had to go all the way back to get them after school was out.

She set her belongings on the gym floor and then unrolled her sleeping bag. It was decorated with a pattern of cute stylized daisies on one side. The other side was a solid pale green that matched the color of her eyes.

She scooched her bag next to a pink glittery one that had to be Aphrodite's. A bright blue bag decorated with math equations lay on the other side of Aphrodite's. Persephone figured it belonged to their brainy friend, Athena. And the red one with the quiver of arrows lying beside it? Artemis's for sure. Another bag covered with question marks was Pandora's, no doubt. She was the most curious girl in the Academy, and was also Athena's roommate.

"Hey, Persephone!" yelled a girl's voice.

"Over here!" called another.

Persephone pushed her long, red curls out of her face and looked across the gym to see Aphrodite, Athena, and Artemis waving her over. She grinned and waved back. Hopping up, she headed toward her three best friends.

They and some other girls were over in the middle of the gym creating silly cheers. Most of those here tonight—like Pandora, Pheme, and Medusa—were on the MOA flag team. But members of the Goddessgirl Squad Cheer team were here tonight too, including Persephone, Athena, Aphrodite, and Artemis.

For a few seconds Persephone stood off to the side

watching the unfamiliar routine the others were doing. Quickly catching on, she joined in the fun, copying the moves and saying the words along with everyone else.

> "Teen Scrollazine *asks:*
>
> *What's your rating?*
>
> *Which godboy is fascinating?*
>
> *Which goddessgirl is glamorous?*
>
> *What do Earth mortals think of us?*
>
> *Woo-hoo!"*

When they finished, some of them did air-splits. Others shook their blue and gold pom-poms or tossed them high. Persephone whooped and clapped.

It was fun being on the GG Squad with her three best friends. Except for Cheer, she wasn't really into sports. Still, she had managed to win the long jump in the first-ever Girls' Olympic Games not long ago. She'd had a good coach. The best. An MOA godboy named Hades.

"I've never heard that cheer before," Persephone commented after she caught her breath.

"Isn't it cool? Pheme just made it up," Pandora told her. She and a bunch of the other girls who'd been doing the cheer were hanging around and chatting nearby.

Hearing her name, Pheme, the goddessgirl of gossip, turned their way. The glittery orange wings Principal Zeus had recently given her rustled softly as she came closer. "Yeah, it was inspired by my reader poll in this week's issue of *Teen Scrollazine*," she said. "In my new column."

The words she spoke puffed in cloud-letters that swiftly rose above her head, and then slowly faded away. Not long ago she'd been caught red-handed snooping around in other girls' rooms. But that hadn't prevented her from landing a new job at the scrollazine. And really, the job of gossip columnist was perfect for the nosiest girl at MOA!

"Awesome," Persephone told Pheme. "About you getting the job and all."

"Thanks." Looking pleased at the praise, Pheme fluffed her short orange hair with her fingers, making it even spikier.

"Want to see the poll?" Pandora asked Persephone. Without waiting for an answer, she dashed over to the sleeping bags on the floor and grabbed a copy of the scrollazine.

Meanwhile, Aphrodite had wandered over to Medusa. From the snippets Persephone overheard, it sounded like Aphrodite was trying to talk the snake-haired girl into letting her do a makeover on her.

Persephone smiled to herself. *Good luck with that,*

Aphrodite! she thought. Medusa was not only snake-headed, with actual live reptiles growing from her head—she could also be hardheaded and superstubborn. And since she wasn't a girly-girl, a makeover didn't seem like anything she'd be interested in.

Couldn't blame Aphrodite for trying, though. She was the goddessgirl of love and *beauty*, after all!

A hand nudged Persephone's arm. Pandora had returned with the issue of *Teen Scrollazine* she'd gone to fetch. When Persephone didn't take it right away, Pheme grabbed it instead and started unrolling it for her.

"I got the brilliant idea of creating a Best of MOA poll," Pheme explained. "So I made up a list of twenty traits, and then asked mortals on Earth to vote on the Mount Olympus Academy student who best fit each trait."

In her enthusiasm, she held the scrollazine super-close to Persephone's face. Persephone drew back a few inches, trying to focus on the words before her eyes.

"Here it is. See?" Pandora helpfully pointed out the poll in Pheme's article.

Persephone took the scrollazine. The quizzes and polls in it were usually silly, harmless fun. Like last week, there had been a poll asking mortals: "If you could have one immortal power, what would you choose?"

The top two answers had been the power to fly and the power to become invisible. Medusa had been disappointed that no one had chosen the power to grow snakes from their head. Of course that wasn't really an immortal power. Medusa was the only one who actually had snake hair, and she was *mortal*.

Quickly Persephone scanned the list of categories and corresponding mortal and immortal MOA students named in this week's scrollazine. They included: Most Academic: Athena; Most Glamorous: Aphrodite;

Best Athlete: Artemis; Most School Spirit: Pandora.

There were boy names mixed in too. Best Musician: Apollo; Most Dramatic: Dionysus; Strongest: Heracles; Handsomest: Ares; Most Fascinating: Hades.

Persephone's eyes lingered on that last one. She found Hades fascinating too!

"I just love polls, don't you?" she heard Pandora ask another girl. Persephone looked up to see that she'd been speaking to Atë, a spirit-goddess who also attended MOA.

Athena, Aphrodite, Artemis, and some other girls had gathered nearby too. "I see some familiar names on this list," Persephone told her three best friends in a teasing voice.

Aphrodite rolled her eyes, smiling. "I know. Ares' head is going to swell big-time when he hears he's handsomest."

She and Ares had an on-again, off-again friendship. For now it was on again, and they seemed to be getting along great. But you never knew from one week to the next how the wind blew with those two.

Unlike them, Persephone and Hades had become good friends almost the minute they'd met. And they'd stayed that way. She stared at the poll, thinking that he would have a very different reaction to finding out he was in it than Aphrodite thought Ares would.

As if reading her mind, Aphrodite asked, "How do you think Hades will feel about the title *he* won in the poll?"

"He'll probably be surprised," said Persephone. "Maybe even a little embarrassed that mortals see him as fascinating. He considers himself serious and gloomy. And he does have a serious job—ruling the Underworld. But, actually, I think that's one of the fascinating things about him!"

The girls around her laughed.

She didn't say so right then, but she also thought there were depths to Hades' character that others sometimes missed. So in her opinion it was nice that mortals considered him fascinating. She agreed with them! She was always learning something new about him. Really, there was no other boy she'd rather hang around with.

Persephone carelessly skimmed the rest of the poll. Other categories included: Best Eyes, Class Clown, Best Hair (Aphrodite again), Most Artistic, Best Smile, and Best Personality. She started to give the 'zine back to Pandora, but then suddenly drew it back. Because she'd spotted her own name!

Most Dependable: Persephone.

Huh? Pink bloomed in her normally pale cheeks. She scrunched her nose as she looked up at her friends. "Dependable?" she asked.

"What's wrong with that? It's a *good* thing," Aphrodite told her.

Artemis nodded. "It means you're a friend we can count on."

"And being chosen shows that mortals love you as much as we do," Athena added. "How could they not?" She gave Persephone a quick hug, seeming to sense her displeasure over the label she'd been given.

But Persephone was having none of her friends' cheery encouragement. *Dependable?* She was not at all flattered by how mortal voters saw her. Not one bit!

Her long hair swayed around her shoulders as she shook her head. "Dependable equals dull and boring," she insisted. "Things like sandals are dependable. You like having them around, but you hardly even notice them."

Her friends exchanged worried glances and shot her looks of concern.

"Everybody notices you," Aphrodite assured her.

"You're awesome," said Athena.

"Yeah, and even if mortals do think you're like sandals, I'm sure they at least think you're the cool silver-winged kind," Artemis piped up.

Persephone couldn't help grinning a little at Artemis's idea of support. Still, she wasn't sure which was worse—being voted Most Dependable or having her friends try so hard to convince her it was a *good* thing. It was like they agreed she was boringly dependable and were trying to make her feel better about accepting the truth.

Good thing the mortals voting in this poll can't hear me now, she thought. *They would vote me Biggest Bad Sport Ever!*

"Sorry," she said softly. "I know I'm being grumpy, but . . ." Her words trailed off. The label she'd been given in this poll was really getting to her. Did everyone at MOA also find her dull, boring, and *dependable*?

"It's a compliment to be mentioned in my poll," Pheme puffed in a lofty voice.

"I know," Persephone said, hoping she hadn't hurt Pheme's feelings. But she couldn't help wondering if everyone at the Academy would soon be thinking: Why would the Most *Fascinating* godboy hang out with the Most *Dependable* goddessgirl? Those two traits did not go together at all.

And what would Hades think? Normally he didn't read *Teen Scrollazine*. Still, he was bound to hear about the poll. His friends would tell him.

"I don't want to hurt your feelings, Pheme, but this poll is totally wrong," someone said. Persephone glanced over her shoulder and saw that it was Medusa who'd spoken. At last, someone who did not think her dependable!

But then Medusa reached up to pat her snakes and said, "I mean, *I* should have gotten Best Hair. Not Aphrodite. It's not fair that she got named for *two* things."

Although Persephone believed her to be wrong in this instance, she admired the way Medusa stuck up for herself. Must be nice to be so confident that you always thought the best of yourself no matter what other people's opinions were. At least, that's how Medusa came across to her.

"Yeah, the poll is totally wrong," Atë agreed. "Because I think I should have gotten Most School Spirit. After all, I *am* a spirit, but Pandora's not."

"Hello? The poll is about having *school* spirit, not about *being* a spirit," argued Pandora. "And don't you think someone who dyes her hair to match MOA's school colors should get voted in for that? Or did you think these blue streaks in my hair were natural?" She bent her head to give everyone a better view of her blue-streaked golden hair.

Athena wrinkled her brow. "Why do we have to label people anyway?" she asked.

"Exactly," said Persephone. She let go of the bottom end of the *Teen Scrollazine* she was holding. It instantly rolled itself shut. *Snap!*

Really, there were two sides to her personality, Persephone thought as she handed the 'zine back to Pandora. A light side and a dark side. Sometimes she was happy and upbeat. The rest of the time, she liked being left alone with her own thoughts. It was ridiculous that others had put *one* label on her! Yet they had. Right there in that poll. She wondered what she could do to change mortals' perception of her.

Suddenly she noticed that a silence had fallen around her. Had her grumpy behavior put a damper on things?

Hey, she was here to have fun tonight, not to have everything ruined by a goofy popularity poll.

Pandora had unrolled the scrollazine again and was rereading the poll on its back cover. Persephone's eyes fell on the front cover, which was facing her way.

Its main headline read: THE ORPHEUS ROCKS THE GODS CONCERT TOUR TO KICK OFF THIS SATURDAY NIGHT! Below that was a picture of a mortal boy rocking out on a stage, with fans crowded around his feet. He had turquoise eyes and thick, spiky brown hair.

"Ooh! Is that Orpheus?" Persephone took the scrollazine back to study the picture on the front page, then turned it toward the group so they could see. "Talk about fascinating! And amazing singing-wise," she added in an awed tone of voice.

She was a huge fan of Orpheus's music, so she truly meant what she said. He was the most popular rock star she knew. Like many MOA students, she even had a poster of him on her bedroom wall.

She'd hoped that changing the subject would lighten everyone's mood. Her ploy worked!

"He's *sooo* cute," Atë agreed, clasping her hands in adoration.

"*Mega*-cute," added Pheme.

"Mega-*dreamy*-cute!" corrected Aphrodite, pretending to swoon over how cute Orpheus was. Then she laughed.

The 'zine poll should've named Aphrodite as having Best Laugh too, thought Persephone. That girl pretty much had it all when it came to attractiveness. Luckily, even though Aphrodite was well aware that she was the most glamorous girl at MOA, she wasn't at all stuck-up about it.

"Apollo loves Orpheus's new song," said Artemis,

peering at the picture of the pop star. Her twin brother, Apollo (voted Best Musician), led a band called Heavens Above that played for all the Academy dances.

"You mean that song 'You A-Muse Me'? My snakes love it too," said Medusa. Everyone stared at her. "What?" she demanded, sounding uncomfortable.

"How do you know they like it?" asked Pandora.

Medusa shrugged. "When they hear it, they boogie. You know. Dance."

There was silence for a few seconds as everyone seemed to be trying to picture that. As most of them knew, Medusa treated her snakes as pets.

"So who's going to the concert tomorrow night?" Persephone asked, changing the subject again. Immediately the hand of every girl in the gym shot into the air.

Unrolling her own copy of *Teen Scrollazine*, another goddessgirl named Iris began reading aloud from the front page article: "'The newest rock sensation is set to perform Saturday night. All of Mount Olympus Academy is invited—both mortal and immortal students.'"

Looking over Iris's shoulder, Pheme read on from where the other girl left off. "'Orpheus is so popular on Earth that mortals named the new Orpheum Theater after him! And he's only thirteen.'"

"Yeah, can you imagine?" said Pandora. "If Orpheus attended MOA, mortals probably would have voted him most fascinating, glamorous, musical, and pretty much everything else in the poll!"

"True!" agreed Aphrodite.

Not wanting to get back on *that* topic again, Persephone searched her mind for another subject to introduce. "Speaking of *truth*, anyone want to play Truth or Dare?"

Ye gods! Why had she said that? Truth or Dare was

far from her favorite game. In her opinion some things were too private for truth. And dares could lead to trouble. But since she was determined to keep steering the conversation away from the poll, the words had popped out of her mouth before she'd been able to come up with something better.

"I'll play!" said Atë excitedly. Ten other girls volunteered too, including Aphrodite and Athena.

"What'll we use for a spinner?" asked Pandora.

"One of my arrows?" suggested Artemis. She trotted over to her sleeping bag and got her quiver. When she returned, she drew out a silver arrow and handed it to the closest girl, which happened to be Persephone. Then, seeming to notice that some of her remaining arrows were dull, Artemis plopped onto the floor and began sharpening their tips.

Persephone dropped cross-legged onto the floor

beside her. The other girls sat too, forming a big circle of a dozen girls, with the arrow in the center.

"Whoever the arrow tip points to after it comes to a stop will be asked 'Truth or Dare,'" Persephone said. With a flick of her wrist, she spun the arrow. When it stopped spinning, its tip was pointing at Athena.

"Oh!" said Athena, looking a bit flustered.

"Truth or Dare?" Persephone asked her.

"Truth," Athena replied.

"Hmm," said Persephone. She tapped her chin with a finger, trying to think of an easy question that wasn't too prying. Finally she asked, "Which of Heracles' Labors did you dislike helping with the most?"

Athena smiled. "Easy one. Cleaning the cattle poop from King Augeas's stables. It was a never-ending and *smelly* job."

Aphrodite wrinkled her nose. "Ick!"

As everyone laughed, Athena leaned forward and spun the arrow. This time it landed on Medusa.

"Truth," Medusa said before Athena could ask her to choose.

"Is it true you gave all of your snakes names?" Athena asked her.

Medusa nodded. When everyone stared at the top of her head curiously, she crossed her arms, getting defensive. "Draw a picture, why don't you?" she said. Although the snakes were preening under the girls' attention, it seemed to make her uncomfortable.

"We're just wondering what their names are," Persephone said gently. "You don't have to tell us, though. It's not required for the game."

"Oh!" Medusa perked up, apparently pleased at their interest now that she realized no one was making fun of her or her snakes. Reaching up, she named each snake on her head, one by one. "Viper, Flicka, Pretzel, Snapper, Twister, Slinky, Lasso, Slither, Scaly, Emerald, Sweetpea, and Wiggle."

After her a few more girls spun the arrow. Some chose truth and others dare, but all were easy challenges.

Then it was Atë's turn. She spun. The arrow was a blur as it whizzed around. When it stopped, its tip was pointing straight at Persephone.

"Truth or Dare," Atë asked her.

Persephone froze. She could see the expectation in everyone's eyes. They thought that good old *dependable* Persephone would choose the "safe" option. They expected her to choose truth. But *was* that really the safest option? Not necessarily. It *depended* on the question.

Her heart raced as she debated what to do. Then,

before she could rethink her choice, the fateful words tumbled from her lips. "Dare. I choose dare."

Too late Persephone recalled that Atë was the spirit of reckless impulse. Spirit-goddesses like her had fewer magical powers than some immortals at MOA, but way more than mortals, who had none at all. Anyway, she was exactly the *wrong* person to ask for a dare.

"Awesome!" Atë rubbed her palms together. Her eyes sparkled with devilish delight as she leaned forward and gleefully spoke. "Persephone, I *dare* you to go up to Orpheus at the concert tomorrow night . . . and get his autograph!"

2

Orpheus Rocks

Hades

THAT SAME FRIDAY NIGHT HADES WAS HANGING out with Apollo, Ares, and some other godboys in the rec room at the end of the boys' dorm hall on the fifth floor of MOA. Right in the middle of laughing at something Apollo said, he suddenly got that prickly feeling on the back of his neck. The one that meant trouble was brewing down in the Underworld.

He hated to go. He was having fun with the guys. They'd been making up funny lyrics to a new tune Apollo had written for his band, Heavens Above.

But duty called, and Hades knew he should leave right away. He needed to find out what was up way down there below the earth. Without a word to anyone, he slipped out of the room and headed downstairs. He was soon outside the Academy, crossing the marble-tiled courtyard.

Overhead the moon was only a thin sliver of white in the night sky. But there were torches burning at the doors of the gym in the distance. He looked over, wondering why the gym was all lit up. There weren't any sports events, drama performances, or parties that he knew of going on there tonight.

Wait a minute. He thought he remembered Persephone saying something about a sleepover with her Cheer team. Something like that, anyway. As he stared, the gym's side door opened. Two shadowy figures went in. They had short hair and broad shoulders.

Were those *boys?* Sneaking into a girls-only sleepover?

Hades immediately switched direction, veering toward the gym. Minutes later he quietly pulled the side door open a few inches and peeked inside. His dark eyes scanned the gym. *Whoa!* There were sleeping bags and girly stuff spread out all over the floor. Lots of girls were sitting or standing around, giggling and chatting in small groups or pairs here and there.

His eyes were drawn to the biggest clump of girls, clustered together in the middle of the gym. He caught a flash of long red curls. Persephone was in that big group! It figured. She was one of the four most popular girls at the Academy, after all. Pretty much everyone liked her. Including him.

As the girls talked, he caught the words *"Teen*

Scrollazine" and "Orpheus." Then suddenly he saw Aphrodite faint. He pulled the door wider, ready to run over and help. Before he could move, however, she straightened again and started laughing. Deciding that everything was okay with the girls after all, he relaxed.

But where were those two sneaky boys? Moving his gaze, he quickly spotted them huddled under the bleachers a couple of dozen feet away. Kydoimos and Makhai. Those jerks were spying on the girls!

Careful not to let anyone see him, Hades stayed close to the wall as he crossed the room. He moved as quietly as a shade—one of the dead from the Underworld. One minute later he was standing right behind the two snoops. As he watched, Kydoimos reached up through the bleachers overhead and snitched a scrollazine that had probably been left there by one of the girls.

"Having fun?" Hades whispered in a sarcastic voice.

Kydoimos and Makhai whipped around, their eyes bugging out in alarm.

Hades jerked his thumb toward the gym door. "Move it. Now."

The three of them managed to slip outside unnoticed by the girls. Hades wasn't sure if it was a breach of school rules for boys to spy on girls, but it certainly wasn't very cool behavior. He didn't really have time to take this matter to Principal Zeus right now, though. So instead he decided to handle things himself. Just like he handled everything in the Underworld.

Once he, Kydoimos, and Makhai were through the door, he spoke a quick chant that would prevent them from returning after he left:

> *"Doors of the gym!*
> *Stay locked up tight.*

Let no boys inside

For the rest of this night."

Then he folded his arms and stared down the two troublemakers, giving them the same stern look he used on misbehaving shades in the Underworld. "Explain yourselves," he commanded. "Or would you like me to report this to Principal Zeus?"

That threat got them talking in a hurry.

"We weren't hurting anyone," whined Makhai. "We were just curious."

Kydoimos nodded. "Don't you ever wonder what girls talk about when we aren't around?"

"No," Hades informed them. "I figure it's their own business. I don't like gossip." Then he added, "I don't like spies, either."

"Oh, really? Then I guess you don't want to know

what us *spies* overheard Persephone say just now," said Makhai.

"Yeah, we won't tell you that she said she's gaga over that mortal rock star Orpheus," said Kydoimos. "Or that she thinks he's 'fascinating.'"

Kydoimos smirked. "I think you've got competition, godboy!" With that, he smacked the 'zine he'd taken from the bleachers against Hades' chest.

Hades automatically clasped the scroll when Kydoimos let go of it. He looked down and saw it was a copy of the newest *Teen Scrollazine*, with a drawing of Orpheus on the cover. When he looked back up again, the other two boys were already walking away.

He angled the cover toward a torch that flamed next to the gym door. In the drawing Orpheus was singing—his latest hit, according to the caption. A bunch of mortal girls were crowded around him cheering. This rock star guy was mega-popular down on Earth. All the MOA girls seemed wild over him too. Even the godboys admired his musical skills. Including Hades.

Normally Hades was a pretty confident guy. Especially when it came to ruling the Underworld. But for some reason what Makhai and Kydoimos had said about Persephone just now made him feel unsettled and maybe even a little jealous.

Of course, that's what those boys wanted. They had hoped to plant the seed of jealousy in him.

He frowned. Well, he wouldn't let the seed grow. So what if Persephone admired Orpheus? That didn't change anything. He could depend on her to be his friend. They understood each other and got along great.

Absently he tugged on the chain he wore around his neck, pulling upward until his fingers closed over the small glass orb that dangled from the chain. Encased within the glass was a single pomegranate seed.

This amulet was a keepsake from the seed-spitting contest Persephone had challenged him to back when they'd first met. It was his good luck charm. He didn't want anyone asking questions about it, though, so he kept it tucked beneath his tunic. Persephone didn't even know about it. No one did. Some things were private.

Speaking of luck, he was going to need some when he reached the Underworld. The back of his neck was prickling big-time now. Which meant the trouble there was getting worse. Quickly he dropped the amulet back inside the neck of his tunic.

"Chariot! Come!" he commanded.

No sooner had he uttered the order than the earth magically opened up before him. *Crack!*

His chariot zoomed out. It was black with gold trim and was drawn by four glossy black stallions. Before it had even touched down, he leaped inside and grabbed the reins. He dropped the *Teen Scrollazine* to the floor of his chariot, never noticing the Best of MOA poll within it.

"To the Underworld!" he shouted.

His horses leaped into the crack in the earth again and magically descended. When he arrived in the Underworld minutes later, Hades was astonished to see a half dozen mortal girls hanging out on the banks of the River Styx.

Spotting his chariot, one of the girls pointed at it. Then the others started jumping up and down and looking excited. To see him?

They were holding signs, he noticed. One of the signs read HADES = HEARTTHROB. Another read HADES = FASCINATING.

Huh? He was no heartthrob. And why would anyone think he was fascinating? What in the Underworld was this all about?

3

Concert Night

Persephone

PERSEPHONE'S OVERNIGHT BAG BUMPED AGAINST her side as she rushed down the hall of the girls' dorm at MOA. It was Saturday, the night of the Orpheus Rocks the Gods concert. Although most girls shared a room, Aphrodite didn't have a roommate. So she'd invited Persephone to spend the night and join in the fun of the pre-concert preparations.

Ever since the big gym sleepover the night before, Persephone had been mega-busy. She'd spent all morning in the Academy greenhouse working on a very important project for Garden-ology class.

After that she'd gone home to help her mom pick flowers from their garden. They'd then delivered them to her mom's store, Demeter's Daisies, Daffodils, and Floral Delights, at the Immortal Marketplace. It was only a few minutes ago that her mom had finally dropped her back at the Academy.

As Persephone headed for Aphrodite's room, she said hi to some other girls who were darting in and out of rooms along the hallway. Many of them had left their doors open tonight. Laughter and excited conversations floated up and down the hall as they helped one another with fashion decisions. Getting ready for big events was a group effort! And it was also more fun this way.

Persephone had just set her overnight bag on Aphrodite's spare bed, and the two girls had exchanged greetings, when Iris and Atë zoomed into the room. After giving them a quick wave, Aphrodite went back to gazing at herself in her mirror and applying makeup.

"Can we borrow some of that flowery perfume you wear?" Iris asked Persephone breathlessly.

"Sure. Let me find it," Persephone replied. She dug through her bag, then pulled out two fancy crystal bottles. One contained a pale purple liquid and the other was filled with a milky white liquid. "Do you want Lavenderlovely or Asphodelight?" she asked.

Iris and Atë both pointed to the pale purple perfume made from crushed lavender petals.

"Lavenderlovely it is!" Smiling, Persephone handed the bottle to the girls. Iris took it with a hurried "Thanks," and then dashed back down the hall. But before Atë followed, she said to Persephone, "Good luck getting Orpheus's autograph tonight!"

"Um, thanks," Persephone replied, smiling weakly. Then the girl was gone.

Before she could get settled and start spiffing herself up, more girls came asking to borrow things. "Persephone, do you have any flowers I could clip in my hair?" "Persephone, can I borrow that flowered scarf?"

Hey! What did they think she was anyway? A store in the Immortal Marketplace? Or maybe they just knew they could count on good old, *dependable* Persephone to have what they needed.

After a while Aphrodite shooed all the borrowers out. "Give the girl time to catch her breath!" she scolded them, but her smile softened her words. Once everyone was gone, she shut the door and went back to standing before the full-length mirror on her closet door.

"You look nice," Persephone told her.

Aphrodite's smile widened, which made her look even more beautiful, if that were possible. She did a dramatic turn to showcase her outfit, causing the skirt of the candy-pink chiton she wore to swirl in the air around her. A thin silver belt decorated with a cluster of hammered silver seashells glittered at her waist. And her long golden hair was threaded with curling ribbons in every shade of pink and red.

Aphrodite's style practically shouted, *Hello. My name is Mega-glamorous!* Persephone thought. That *Teen Scrollazine* poll was right. The word "glamorous" fit her as perfectly as that chiton. She always seemed so certain of her fashion choices, and those choices always made her look effortlessly amazing.

Persephone opened her bag, grabbed one of the four chitons she'd brought, and went to stand before the other full-length mirror on Aphrodite's spare closet door. She held the pale green chiton against her chest and gazed at her reflection. The style and color of the chiton was kind of . . . expected.

Did her own personal style shout, *Hello. My name is Dependable?* Well, it wouldn't tonight! she decided firmly. Going back to the bed, she balled up the chiton and stuffed it back into her bag.

Though she liked clothes, she usually didn't think too much about her fashion choices. But earlier this afternoon she'd felt uncharacteristically unsure about what she should wear to the concert as she'd packed her overnight bag at home.

Because the *Teen Scrollazine* poll results had upset her, she'd brought way too much stuff. Now she laid it all out on the spare bed and stared at it.

Hmm. What would a not-so-dependable girl wear to a concert? she wondered.

From the corner of her eye, she watched Aphrodite slick on a glittery pink lip gloss. She didn't want to mimic her awesome friend's style. But she did want to try out a new style of her own. Tonight would be a fresh start. A whole new look for a new her.

She poked around uncertainly in the mound of clothes she'd brought.

"Can't decide what to wear?" Aphrodite asked.

Persephone glanced over at her. "Well, I was thinking of a garden theme. Leaves, flowers."

"Ooh! That sounds cute!" said Aphrodite.

A knock came at the door. It opened, and Athena stood there, looking a bit frazzled. "Fashion emergency. Aphrodite, could you come help?"

"Sure, I'm pretty much ready," said Aphrodite. "But what's wrong? You look fab as you are."

Athena did look cute. The hem of her blue chiton was

scalloped and edged with a band of darker blue that was a perfect match for the clasps in her long wavy brown hair. Although she usually didn't wear much makeup, tonight she'd added a pale blue shadow on her eyelids.

"Thanks, but the emergency isn't me," said Athena. "It's Artemis. She's trying to choose the perfect outfit to match her new arrow quiver. Which is the color of mud. And which she's planning to bring to the concert."

Aphrodite's brows rose. "Why would she do that?"

Athena shrugged, making an *I have no clue* face.

"Maybe because she takes it everywhere?" Persephone chimed in.

"True," said Athena. "Only this time I was hoping we could talk her out of it."

"Okay, I'm on it," said Aphrodite, heading for the door. She glanced back at Persephone. "Unless *you* need help?"

Persephone picked up a bright yellow chiton from the

bed and smiled at her friends. "No, I'm okay. You go on."

Once Aphrodite and Athena were out of the room, Persephone shut the door behind them and flew into action. She pulled on the yellow chiton, which was edged with a leafy garland design. Then she tugged on ivy-green sandals that laced up her calves. So far, so good.

Next she pulled out two pairs of earrings. One pair featured delicate dangly green leaves. The other was a pair of yellow daisy studs. She held the two pairs up on either side of her face and gazed in the mirror. *Hmm. Which pair looked less dependable?*

Suddenly she got a brilliant idea. She put a daisy stud in her left ear, but in her right ear she hung a single dangly leaf earring.

Persephone stared at the effect in Aphrodite's mirror. What would everyone think of her unmatched earrings? she wondered. She tossed her head, causing the dangly leaf to sway. *Who cares?* she decided. Maybe they'd think they couldn't *depend* on her to look the same anymore!

Getting more and more excited, she decided to go all out with her new undependable look. Time for makeup.

Each dorm room had two desks, and Aphrodite had converted her spare one to a makeup table. It was covered with an incredible variety of neatly arranged, color-coded makeup. There were rows and rows of nail polish and lip glosses in every conceivable color, all lined up on a silver tray. Plus dozens of little pots of eye shadow, blush, and creams. It was like a mini cosmetics shop!

Persephone sat in the desk chair and considered what to try. Getting an idea, she tapped a fingertip on a long, slender box. It popped open, and a magical makeup brush flew out to hover in midair just a few inches from her nose.

"Can you paint a flower on my face?" she asked it.

The brush did a little flip as if delighted by the unusual idea. Quickly it zipped down to the tray of colors, which Aphrodite had left open. Then it zoomed up to Persephone's cheek.

As it got to work, Persephone grabbed a few of Aphrodite's old *Teen Scrollazines* and hurriedly flipped through them. When she came to a sketch of a girl whose hair was long and wavy, she paused. It was similar to her own style. Only this girl's hair was way wilder. It looked awesome!

The makeup brush finished its job in no time at all. Persephone's hand shook a little in nervous anticipation as she lifted Aphrodite's silver-backed hand mirror. At the sight of her reflection, she gasped.

There were several glittery daisies—orange, yellow, and white—painted on her left cheekbone. Small green leaves and curling tendrils were tucked into the arrangement here and there. The glittery flowers went great with her skin, which already had the soft, natural shimmer that all immortals got from drinking nectar.

"It's perfect!" she breathed. She smiled at the brush. "Thank you!"

The brush bent its bristly tips toward her as if taking a bow. Then it zoomed back to its box. Once it was tucked inside, the box's lid snapped shut again.

Now for her hairstyle. Gazing into Aphrodite's hand mirror again, Persephone softly chanted, "Magic mirror, let me see . . . How would this hairstyle look on me?"

As her words died away, she touched the sketch she'd admired in the scrollazine to the center of the mirror. Almost immediately she felt her hair begin to move, magically rearranging itself into a style that matched the sketch.

When she pulled the sketch away, she gazed into the mirror. Her hair looked amazing. It was still long, but now it was lustrously thick and kind of wild. She loved it! But it needed a little . . . something.

She jumped up and fetched some decorative leafy garlands she'd brought in her bag. Standing before the big mirror on Aphrodite's closet door, she tossed the greenery into the air overhead.

"Thread through my hair, oh garland green,
In the cutest way that's ever been seen."

As the garlands fell toward her, they began to thread themselves into her hair. Just as the last garland slid into place, she heard the door open behind her.

She whirled around in time to see Athena, Aphrodite, and Artemis enter the room. With a hopeful smile on her face, she struck a dramatic pose like she'd once seen a fashion model do in the Immortal Marketplace. Her hair swung smoothly, brushing low to almost cover the left half of her face in what felt like a mysterious and *undependable* style.

"What do you think?" she asked her three friends.

She was excited to show off her new look. But at the same time she was a tiny bit worried. Because it would squash her enthusiasm if they didn't like what she'd done.

Aphrodite's and Athena's eyes widened. Artemis tilted her head to one side, appearing confused.

After a small silence Aphrodite said, "I think you look a*dor*able!"

"I agree," said Athena. "The face paint is mega-original, and your hair is darling!"

"You look like a different person," said Artemis. She didn't sound like this was necessarily a good thing. But then she smiled and added, "I could get used to it, though."

Persephone gave a sigh of relief. Though her friends seemed a little taken aback by her new look, they were also supportive of her desire to try something new.

"You all look fantastic!" she told them in return. "I love that red chiton on you, Artemis."

Artemis preened, seeming pleased. "Thanks."

Persephone noticed that she wasn't carrying her quiver. Aphrodite and Athena must've succeeded in talking her out of it. And if she wasn't mistaken, the chiton Artemis had on was one of Aphrodite's. Aphrodite had so many clothes that she kept some of them in Artemis's spare closet. She'd obviously convinced Artemis to try this chiton on—and keep it on.

"Last one to the concert is a rotten egg!" someone called from the hallway.

"Let's hit the road," said Aphrodite, her blue eyes sparkling.

Wildly excited about the fun they were going to have, the four goddessgirls dashed from the room.

4

Starstruck

Persephone

After just a few steps down the hall, Persephone stumbled, very nearly falling in. The left side of her hair kept flopping over her face, making it hard to see where she was going. But it was worth it to look so different. Tonight she was breaking out of her dependable box! She just hoped she didn't trip and break her neck in the process.

Just before they reached the stairs to head down, she skidded to a halt. "Oops! I almost forgot." She turned and darted back into Aphrodite's room.

There she quickly pulled a small sheet of blank papyrus and an ink-filled feather pen from her overnight bag. Finding the drawstring purse she'd brought that matched her dress, she stashed everything inside it. She was going to need this stuff to get Orpheus's autograph. *If* she dared to follow through with Atë's dare!

Outside in the Academy's courtyard a fleet of chariots was waiting to take everyone to the concert. The MOA logo and a thunderbolt were emblazoned on the side of each chariot. Principal Zeus had ordered enough transport to carry the entire student body.

Persephone's friends called her over to the silver chariot they'd chosen to ride in. It had four pink seats and was hitched to three silver unicorns. Aphrodite quickly put a spell over the chariot, so their hairstyles wouldn't be blown around by the wind as they flew.

Soon the goddessgirls were departing the Academy, which stood atop Mount Olympus, the highest mountain in Greece. With a burst of speed their chariot whooshed upward. Artemis held the reins, guiding the unicorns as they soared through a cloudless blue-black sky. Stars sparkled overhead like diamonds. It was a magical night.

Still, as they drew closer to their destination, Persephone grew tense. How was she going to get Orpheus to sign her papyrus?

Ever since last night, she'd been imagining various scenarios. Like lying in wait for him in his dressing room at intermission. Or catapulting herself onto the stage after the show. Each method she considered seemed impossible, terrifying, or embarrassing. Or all three at once!

"Right, Persephone?" she suddenly heard Athena ask.

"Huh?" Persephone looked at her friends, wondering what she'd missed.

"We were just saying that you don't really have to do that dumb dare from the sleepover," said Artemis.

"No one will care if you don't get Orpheus's autograph," Athena told her kindly.

"I know that," said Persephone. Honestly! Did her friends think she wasn't daring enough to follow through on a dare?

Should she do it, though? After all, she usually *did* follow through on things. So if she got the autograph tonight, would it actually mean she'd made the *dependable* choice? The exact opposite of the kind of choice she wanted to make? *Phew!* This was getting confusing!

"Atë shouldn't have given you such a hard dare to do anyway," Aphrodite went on. "In Truth or Dare the dares are supposed to be things you can do right away during the game."

"I'm not worried. It'll be fun," Persephone insisted, knowing she was sealing her fate. She smiled brightly even though it was giving her a stomachache to even think about approaching a mega-pop star like Orpheus.

All too soon the MOA chariots were landing on the lawn in front of the new Orpheum Theater in Greece. Torchlights gleamed everywhere. Out in front of the theater there was a huge marquee:

PREMIERING TONIGHT:

THE ORPHEUS ROCKS THE GODS

CONCERT TOUR!

Dozens of MOA students were already streaming inside for the concert. Immortal students from other schools around the world had been invited as well. The four goddessgirls joined the throng, heading for the stairs that led up to the theater.

"I wonder if Ares is here yet," Aphrodite said, looking around. "He and some of the guys are hoping to catch Orpheus either before or after the concert and maybe pick up some music tips from him."

Persephone walked ahead of her friends a little, her eyes scanning the crowd for Hades. She didn't see him. He often missed classes to take care of Underworld business, and he'd been busy there all day today. Still, she hoped he wasn't so swamped in the Underworld that he'd miss out on tonight.

When Athena said something behind her, Persephone turned to look at her. Unfortunately, her new hairstyle caused her red hair to swing into her face again.

Oof! She bumped into someone in front of her.

"Oops! Sorry," she said, stepping back. "I wasn't watching where I was going."

"No problem," a voice replied. A boy's voice. It was as smooth as silk. Almost musical. Something about it made Persephone's spirits rise.

She pushed her hair out of her face to see who the voice belonged to. *Ye gods!* The boy she had run into was none other than Orpheus himself!

The show would start in mere minutes. So what was he doing outside the theater? She'd certainly never expected to see him out here mixing with the crowd.

Stunned, she could only stare, wide-eyed, and stammer. "Oh, uh, um."

And then the rock star was moving off, rushing toward a girl with bright pink hair, who was wearing dozens and dozens of bracelets on her arms. "Eurydice!" he called.

All at once Persephone's three friends were by her side. "Wow! Was that—," Aphrodite began.

"Orpheus?" Athena finished.

Persephone nodded. And like an idiot she'd just missed her big chance to get that autograph!

"There you are, E!" Orpheus was saying to the pink-haired girl up ahead. "You're late. I was worried you wouldn't show."

The girl just giggled and playfully tapped her fingers on his shoulder. "Don't be such a worrywart, O. I was getting dressed and lost track of time. So how do I look? White-and-black-tastic, don't you think?"

She twirled around, showing off the unusual chiton she wore. The entire left half of it was black and its right side was white. A dramatic black-and-white feather boa floated around her shoulders too.

And just like Persephone, she was wearing mismatched earrings. She'd gone even further, though. She was also wearing mismatched sandals! They were both the same style. However, one was black and one was white.

"Forgive me?" the girl asked Orpheus in a teasing voice. She batted her eyes, and Persephone could see that they were outlined in thick swirls drawn in black and white too.

Orpheus smiled at the girl, flashing his perfect teeth. "Natch."

Wow! thought Persephone. This pink-haired girl was the opposite of dependable, in her opinion. She'd even dared to arrive late to hang out with the biggest mega-pop star on Earth!

Plus, although the various pieces she wore appeared casually thrown together, they *worked*. Talk about personal style! Persephone yearned to be like her. She studied the girl closely, feeling as dazzled by her as Orpheus appeared to be.

"I think that girl is O's—I mean, Orpheus's— girlfriend," said Aphrodite. As the goddess of love, she had a sixth sense about who liked who. Not that a sixth sense was needed to see that Orpheus and this girl liked one another. It was obvious!

"Her name is Eurydice," said Pheme. Her sudden appearance made Persephone jump in surprise. With the help of her new wings, the orange-haired goddess-girl had suddenly whooshed up out of nowhere to stand beside them.

Pheme's sixth sense involved the uncanny ability to know when you wanted information about someone else. And she often managed to come along at the exact right moment to supply the specific info you wanted. Like now.

"She's touring as backup singer for Orpheus," Pheme went on in her usual puff-speak. "And you know his hit song, 'You A-Muse Me'?"

"You a-muse me, confuse me . . . O, will your heart bruise meee-ee-ee? Oh, yeah!" crooned a girl's voice from behind Pheme. Medusa had come over too. Now she sang a little more of the well-known refrain.

A small surprised silence fell among the girls. Medusa could actually sing! And her snakes were boogying to the beat, just like she'd said they sometimes did. Weird!

Medusa stopped singing and looked at Pheme. "So? You were saying?"

Pheme smiled at her. The two of them were friends and often ate in the cafeteria together with Pandora. Persephone figured they'd come in the same chariot too.

"Yeah, anyway. So Orpheus believes Eurydice is his muse," Pheme went on. "Lots of his songs are rumored to be written about her. Including that hit Medusa just sang." She elbowed the snake-haired girl good-naturedly. "Good singing, by the way."

"Thanks," said Medusa.

Up ahead a muscular boy with a tattoo of a cobra on his arm walked up to Orpheus and Eurydice. Persephone noticed that his tattoo kept changing shape and realized it must be a magical removable one like those she'd once seen for sale in the Immortal Marketplace. Made sense, because she didn't know anyone their age with a permanent tattoo.

"We'd better get moving," the tattooed boy told Orpheus and Eurydice. His eyes narrowed as he studied everyone and everything in the surrounding area, like he was checking for hidden dangers. Seeming satisfied that all was safe for the moment, he accompanied Orpheus and Eurydice as the trio headed for the back of the theater.

"Who's that boy?" asked Athena.

"Orpheus's bodyguard," Pheme informed them.

Bodyguard! Persephone hadn't considered that obstacle. If Orpheus's security guard tagged along the rest of the night, that might make getting an autograph impossible. She wasn't sure whether or not to be glad about that.

"His name's Viper," Pheme continued. "Because he always wears different snake tattoos."

At her mention of the bodyguard's name, one of Medusa's snakes stood up straight from her head. When it shaped itself into a question mark, Medusa must've somehow realized it because she grinned. "No, Viper, she's not talking about you," she told the snake, reaching up to give it a pat.

Ta-ta-ta-tah! Two heralds had come to stand at the top of the theater steps. They were blowing on long slender trumpets called salpinxes to summon everyone inside. At the sound the girls hurried into the theater. The concert was about to start!

Inside, stone benches were arranged in semicircular rows facing the stage, which was raised about four and a half feet off the floor. Although the theater was filling up with of immortals (and a few mortals, too), there was still space in an area in front of the stage where there were no seats.

"Let's go up front," said Aphrodite, nudging Athena, Artemis, and Persephone forward.

Minutes later the curtain rose. And there stood Orpheus. Center stage. A roar went up from the crowd.

Strumming his tortoiseshell lyre, he started right in, rocking the theater. Most lyres had no more than eight strings. Apollo's had seven. But Orpheus's lyre was specially made with twelve. No one else in history had been able to play such a complicated instrument. Soon the entire audience was dancing and singing along to the beat.

Even Persephone, who was sometimes too self-conscious to participate, got caught up in the music. She and her friends rocked out when Orpheus and his band played a fast song. During slow songs they swayed and twirled gracefully.

Copying her friends, Persephone raised her hands toward the stage, curving her fingers together to make a heart shape. They wanted to show Orpheus how much they *loved* his music. When he finished one of their favorite tunes, the four best goddessgirl friends hugged in excitement, jumping around.

"This is the best concert ever!" Artemis squealed. Which made them all laugh because normally Artemis wasn't the type of girl to squeal. Ever.

Persephone was having a fabulous time! But every now and then she would remember the dare, and in those moments her enjoyment would dim a little. If only she could figure out an easy and unembarrassing way to get that autograph!

Finally, when she judged that the concert was nearing its end, she decided it was now or never. She slipped away from her friends and began inching closer to the stage. Though it was only a few yards ahead, the crowd was so packed that it was slow going. It seemed that dozens of other girls had the same idea and were jostling to get in position to ask for autographs the minute the concert ended.

When Persephone was just a few feet from her goal, Eurydice joined Orpheus up onstage for a final duet. Down in the pit the crowd's excitement rose to a fevered pitch. Persephone was rocked this way and that.

Without warning she found herself pressed against the front edge of the raised stage. As the duet came to an end, the crowd surged forward, pressing her even harder. Her eyes were on a level with Orpheus's sandals. Her heart was pounding. This was getting dangerous. She felt like she was about to be crushed!

Then suddenly, from somewhere behind her, a pair of strong hands landed on either side of her waist. She found herself being lifted high above the crowd. Rescued! All at once Orpheus reached down to her and pulled her to stand beside him onstage.

"Hi there, flower girl," he quipped, noting the daisies on her cheek. Excited whispers and gasps came from the girls in the audience behind her. They probably all wished they were in her sandals right now.

But Persephone's mind was on one thing, and one thing only. She looked up at Orpheus. Stared right into his sparkly turquoise eyes. Then she blurted, "Can I have your autograph?"

The whole theater burst out laughing. She glanced over her shoulder at the crowd, but it was hard to see beyond the bright torches that ringed the stage.

"Why are they laughing?" Persephone murmured. She flipped her hair out of her face and looked at the pink-haired Eurydice, who was standing nearby.

"The acoustics in the theater are perfect," Eurydice whispered. "So whoever speaks onstage can be heard from any seat. And they're not laughing *at* you, sweets," she went on. "They think you were making a joke. Maybe you didn't realize it, but Orpheus and I were just singing one of his hit songs. The one called 'Can I Have Your Autograph?'"

Persephone blushed. "And then I asked . . . Oh, I get it now."

Meanwhile, Orpheus had turned toward the crowd. He egged them on, saying: "What do you think? Should I give the flower girl an autograph?"

Everyone in the crowd clapped and cheered enthusiastically. "Yes! Yes!" they shouted.

"Well, I *would*, but it seems I don't have a pen or any papyrus," Orpheus continued, playing up to the audience.

"I do," Persephone volunteered. Only, then she realized she actually didn't. In the crush a minute ago, she'd dropped her drawstring purse. "Um, I *did*, that is. Wait! I know—I'll use my magic to make what I need. Just a sec."

"Um . . ." She fumbled to think of the spell she needed to create the stuff Orpheus had requested. It was an easy spell. She'd learned it way back in second grade, for godness' sakes! Still, she just stood there, her mind a blank. It was overwhelming being so close to these two megastars. And unlike them, she didn't really enjoy being the center of attention like this.

Hurriedly she mumbled what she thought was the right spell. But instead of papyrus and a feather pen, only the pen appeared in her hands. It seemed she'd gotten the spell half right at least.

Unsure what to do now, she presented the pen to Orpheus. He laughed and sent a cocky grin toward the audience. Taking the pen, he lifted her hand in his until her arm was outstretched between them. Then, with a dramatic flourish, he wrote his name on her forearm.

Persephone stared at her arm in surprise. He'd autographed it! His name was huge, going all the way from the inside of her elbow to her wrist.

"Um, thank you," she told him.

"You're welcome, flower girl." With that, Orpheus

gave her a quick light kiss on the cheek. All the girls in the audience sighed in delight.

Eurydice rolled her eyes and grinned at the crowd. "What a flirt!" she said.

And then the two stars launched into an encore duet of another of Orpheus's hit songs. Fittingly, it was the one called "What a Flirt!"

To accompany it, they did an impromptu skit in which Orpheus pretended to sing his song to Persephone and Eurydice pretended to get jealous. It was all done in fun, of course. And the crowd loved it.

In spite of being in the limelight—or under the stage lights, actually—Persephone started to relax. Tonight was working out great. Not only had she finished the dare and gotten the autograph, she was hanging out with the biggest pop stars on Earth!

5

Fascinating

Hades

*C*RACK! IT WAS SATURDAY NIGHT WHEN Hades' stallions pushed up from the Underworld and landed his chariot in front of the Orpheum Theater. He leaped down. On his command the chariot and horses quickly disappeared back into the ground.

Ta-ta-ta-tah! He'd arrived just as the heralds were

sounding their salpinxes. The Orpheus Rocks the Gods concert was about to begin!

Hades' eyes searched the crowd streaming into the theater. Having gotten here late, he'd had to land a distance away from it. Dozens of other chariots were already parked all around the theater, and the deer, unicorns, and horses that had pulled them were grazing nearby.

Way up ahead he glimpsed Persephone and her friends at the top of the theater steps. He raced to catch up, but lost sight of them as they entered the Orpheum.

"Drat," he muttered. He'd been hoping to hang out with Persephone before the concert. He wanted to ask her advice on how to handle those mortal girls hanging around the River Styx. She was good at helping him think things through sometimes. Unfortunately, he'd gotten here too late to talk to her.

"Hades!" a voice called out.

He turned to see three members of Heavens Above—Apollo, Ares, and Dionysus—bringing one of the MOA chariots in for a landing. The only band member missing was Poseidon, Hades' roommate, who was godboy of the sea. He'd gone to investigate a shipwreck in the Mediterranean Sea.

Hades jogged over to them. Their chariot was flashy, with sides in deep purple, and an enormous gold thunderbolt on the front. Principal Zeus had gone all out with his transportation arrangements.

Apollo was the first one to hop out. "Hurry," he urged the others. "We need seats close to the stage if we want to catch Orpheus after the concert."

"Catch him?" Hades echoed. He fell in step with the other godboys, and they all headed for the theater.

"Mr. Limenius said we could invite Orpheus to

MOA for the week," Ares informed him.

"To sit in on our Music-ology classes," Dionysus added. "And maybe give a concert or two with our band while he's there."

"Awesome, right?" said Apollo. Then, as if just remembering something, he sent Hades a questioning glance. "If he agrees, can I count on you to sit in on drums while Poseidon's gone?"

Before Hades could reply, some goddessgirls he didn't recognize from another school walked by.

"Look! It's that *fascinating* Hades! And that *handsome* Ares," he overheard them say. Then they giggled and moved on.

Huh? He didn't even know them. Come to think of it, though, those mortal girls hanging out at the River Styx had called him "fascinating" too. And they'd kept asking him to autograph their *Teen Scrollazine*s. He'd ignored their requests, of course, sternly banishing them all from the riverbank.

But now, as the godboys headed up the steps to the theater, Hades looked over at Ares and cocked his head toward the two girls. "What's up with that?"

"Haven't you seen the poll in the new *Teen Scrollazine*?" asked Dionysus.

Hades shook his head.

Ares whipped out a folded piece of papyrus from his pocket. Grinning, he handed it to Hades, saying, "Prepare to be wowed, godboy."

The two of them had been enemies at the start of the year. As the godboy of war, Ares could be hotheaded. But they eventually had come to an understanding, thanks to Persephone's help. Now they were good enough friends to joke around and hang out together. Most of the time, anyway.

Hades unfolded the papyrus. It was an article torn from this week's issue of the scrollazine. Some kind of list. He scanned it, and found his name.

Looking on, Apollo laughed good-naturedly. "So how does it feel to be voted the most fascinating godboy at MOA?" Then he hooked his thumb toward Ares. "Mr. Handsomest here is carrying that article around like it's an award. Can you believe this guy?"

"Well, this explains a lot," said Hades, handing the article back to Ares. "There were a bunch of girls hanging around the Underworld yesterday. With signs and hearts and stuff."

Ares grinned and clapped him on the back as they reached the top of the steps. "We're officially girl magnets, god-dude. Face it."

And then they were inside the theater. "I seriously doubt those girls hanging around the river would find me fascinating if they knew the dull, humdrum things I do in the Underworld," Hades insisted as they made their way toward seats. "Like calming down whiny shades. Not to mention dealing with the Furi—"

He broke off midsentence when he caught sight of a yellow chiton in the crowd. Persephone. Maybe he could catch up with her after the concert and get her advice on the situation back at the River Styx.

Keeping an eye on her, he followed the guys as they found seats several rows back from the stage. As the curtain rose, they settled in to enjoy the show. Turned out that Orpheus was an even more amazing singer and musician in person!

Toward the end of the concert, Hades noticed that Persephone was moving through the crowd down below. She'd left her friends and was heading for the stage on her own. When a ripple of excitement swept the audience, the adoring fans around her started rushing forward to get closer to the rock stars onstage.

Hades leaped to his feet. He had to *do* something. Persephone could be crushed down there! Without a word to the other godboys, he pushed his way through the concertgoers, heading straight for her.

"Persephone!" he shouted. Of course, she couldn't hear him above the roar of the music and the shouts from the crowd.

As people swelled closer to the stage, she glanced over her shoulder for a second. There was a panicky look on her face that made his heart pound with fear for her safety. Though it felt like it took forever, he surged ahead and reached her within seconds.

Quickly he put his hands on either side of her waist and lifted her high and clear of danger. He'd intended to set her on one of his shoulders and then plow back through the crowd, returning her to her friends. But all of a sudden she was pulled from his hands. And then she was onstage!

Orpheus had reached down for her at the very same moment Hades had lifted her up. Then he'd hauled her to stand between Eurydice and him at the edge of the stage.

Persephone didn't even seem to realize that Hades had been the one to give her a boost up. Not that she needed to thank him for saving her, but still.

He watched as Orpheus teased her, to the delight of the crowd. It was all in fun. No big deal. But then that smiley pop star autographed her arm. And gave her a kiss!

Whoa! Hades had never even given her a kiss before. He folded his arms, glowering a little.

Then he got that prickling feeling on the back of his neck again. *Drat!* There must be more trouble down in the Underworld.

He gazed up at Persephone onstage. It didn't matter if she knew he'd been the one to rescue her. The important thing was that she was safe. And he had work to do. So . . . fun over.

Once he was outside the theater, he summoned Midnight, his favorite black stallion. After the sleek horse magically appeared, he mounted it and swiftly descended belowground.

When Hades finally reached the Underworld, he could hardly believe his eyes. He'd banished all the mortal fangirls from the riverbank just last night. Yet here they were, back again. And now there were way more of them hanging out by the river than before. They were everywhere.

Some were picnicking on the bank of the River Styx. A few were even wading in the shallows. Several were arguing with Charon, the moody old boat captain who'd had the job of ferrying the dead to the Underworld for, like, *ever*. It looked as if they were nagging him to give them a ride across the river!

Hades swooped toward them on Midnight. The girls went wild when they saw him land on the riverbank alongside the docked ferryboat. Many were holding signs that said things like: WE ♥ HADES, THE UNDERWORLD IS *HOT*! or MEMBERS OF THE OFFICIAL MR. FASCINATING FANGIRLS CLUB.

"Can we have a tour of the Underworld?" one girl shouted out to him. "We'd love to see what you do down here," called another. "It would be *sooo fascinating*." Several girls giggled at the mention of that word from the 'zine poll.

"No!" he said. "Are you all crazy? The Underworld is a treacherous place. Everywhere you look there are swamps or rivers of lava. And did you hear about my giant three-headed dog, Cerberus? You do not want to mess with him."

But try as he might, Hades couldn't make these girls understand all that. *Or* the fact that although it was okay for immortals to visit the Underworld now and then, it was *not* okay for mortals to.

"Do something!" Charon told him, sounding alarmed. "It's been like this all day. Not-dead girls trying to trick me into taking them to the Underworld." He scratched his head. "Don't know quite what to make of it."

"Don't worry. They'll forget all about me when the new issue of *Teen Scrollazine* comes out next week," Hades assured Charon in grim tones. Still, a week seemed a long way off at the moment.

"Humph! Well, I'm not the only one who's had enough of this excitement." Charon pointed upward.

Hades' gaze followed the boat captain's finger.

Uh-oh. The three flying Furies—Alecto, Megaera, and Tisiphone—were circling overhead. Somehow they'd gotten wind of what was going on here. And they did not look happy.

Although Hades ruled the Underworld, these ladies were the judges who decided punishments for rule-breakers in special cases. Cases that would include any mortals who tried to trick their way in.

If these girls crossed the river and set one foot in the Underworld, the Furies would make sure they'd be stuck there. Forever!

6

Deeds of Friendship

Persephone

Persephone hummed one of Orpheus's songs as her hands broke up clumps of soil in a planting tray. She was standing before her worktable in the Gardenology greenhouse, just off the MOA courtyard near the olive grove that Athena had created earlier in the year.

It was Monday afternoon, fourth period, and she was working on a class assignment. Her teacher Ms. Thallo had tasked each student in the class with creating a completely new, never-before-seen hybrid plant of some kind.

If Persephone's worked out as she hoped, she planned to give it to Hades. It was perfect timing because this coming Saturday was his birthday. And she wanted to give him a gift that no one else but she could create. Something beautiful that would lighten his heart whenever things in the Underworld got him down.

All last week she'd experimented with mixing various kinds of flower species together. It wasn't easy making a plant hardy enough to survive the heat and bleakness of the Underworld.

Her failed efforts so far were lined up against the glass wall of the greenhouse near her worktable. Droopy daisy-daffodil hybrids. Limp lavender-lily-lilacs. Sad-looking snapdragon-sunflowers.

But today she was going to try mixing seeds from *four* different flowering species. Her tray was filled ten inches deep with soil she'd sneaked out of the Underworld in a bag last week. After smoothing the soil, she scooped out a hole just the right size.

When all was ready, she cupped four different kinds of seeds in her palms. Curling her fingers, she clenched the seeds tight between both hands. The use of magic wasn't permissible for every assignment, but it was for this one. So, standing in front of the tray, she drew a deep breath and uttered a magical chant:

> *"Chrysanthemum, cactus,*
>
> *Protea, rose,*
>
> *Please mix together*
>
> *And show me what grows!"*

Within her hands she felt the four seeds shrink and combine themselves into one teardrop-size seed. She pressed the new single seed into the bed of soil and covered it over.

A pale green shoot sprang from the bed right away. In seconds it became a sturdy green stalk. Leaves sprouted. The stalk grew taller. And then a single bud appeared. At first its petals were clinched tightly shut. But then they began to unfurl.

And much to her delight, an amazing flower bloomed. It was enormous, measuring about twelve inches across, with bright pink and orange petals and a pale yellow center.

"How's your project going?" her teacher asked.

Persephone looked up from her worktable to see Ms. Thallo at her side. Her skin was as dark as the soil in the planting tray, and long, curling vines of ivy grew from her head. She was Persephone's favorite teacher.

"Pretty well," Persephone replied in answer to her question. She gestured toward the flower she'd created. "I cultivated the seeds for my new plant variety and designed them to grow at whatever speed I command.

"It's a variation of the King Protea flower," Persephone went on as Ms. Thallo examined the blossom from all angles. "Combined with chrysanthemum, cactus, and rose."

"A daring choice," her teacher said with approval. Although Ms. Thallo couldn't have known, this particular description of Persephone's choice of seeds thrilled her.

"However, proteas won't grow in the gardens of Mount Olympus. Or in many places on Earth for that matter," Ms. Thallo commented. "They thrive in extremely hot climates."

"Which is perfect!" said Persephone. "Because I'm going to plant my hybrid down in the Underworld. To brighten up the gloom a bit."

The teacher blinked at her. Still looking dubious, she said, "An admirable goal. But the heat there at times may be too much even for the protea. No flower has ever managed to survive in the Underworld, except the asphodel."

Persephone touched one of her new flower's orange petals. "This blossom is designed to flourish in extreme heat. Even in fire. At least I hope it will. Since my test run went okay here in the greenhouse just now, I'm going to make more of my new seeds. I'll take them to the Underworld after school today, plant them, and command them not to blossom till next Saturday. I'm hoping if they take more time growing, it'll increase their chances of survival."

Ms. Thallo clapped her hands together like she sometimes did when she was excited. "It will be intriguing to see if so beautiful a blossom can actually thrive in the Underworld. It's the ultimate inhospitable environment!" She beamed at Persephone. "I can always depend on you to come up with an idea that amazes."

Persephone sighed inwardly as Ms. Thallo moved away. There was that word again. "Depend," as in "*depend*able." She'd liked it better when the teacher had described her work as *daring*.

Ms. Thallo's ivy hair swayed, gently rustling as she turned back to gaze at Persephone thoughtfully. "In fact, if your Underworld test succeeds," she said, "I think you should consider entering your hybrid in the Anthestiria Flower Festival."

Persephone's green eyes widened. "Really?" Her voice rose to an excited squeak.

Ms. Thallo nodded. "Really. Your new flower is quite extraordinary."

"Okay, I'll think about it," she said as the teacher left the greenhouse to return to the Garden-ology classroom in the main Academy building. Getting a flower accepted into the Anthestiria festival was an honor bestowed on only a lucky few. It was super-complimentary of Ms. Thallo to suggest that Persephone should enter her project.

The festival was held just once every four years and took place on the island of Cyprus, near Greece. One of the highlights was a flower parade with decorated floats. Closing her eyes for a moment, Persephone imagined an Underworld-themed float showcasing her new flower. Maybe she could design a dress out of the petals from her flowers to wear in the parade too. How awesome would that be?

But enough daydreaming. She had work to do!

She spent the rest of class creating more hybrid seeds.

When the lyrebell rang, she placed them in a small box, which she stowed in her scrollbag. Then, hearing a commotion outside in the courtyard, she pushed open the greenhouse door and scurried out.

A Hermes' Delivery Service chariot was landing in the courtyard. But instead of his usual load of packages, Hermes carried Orpheus and Eurydice today! Persephone stopped short, barely able to believe her eyes. Except for a few other students scattered across the courtyard, hardly anyone was around to see the rock stars arrive.

Orpheus's bodyguard was standing on the ledge at the back of the chariot, holding on and surveying the courtyard. He acted like he expected evildoers and villains to jump out and attack at any moment.

Calm down, Viper, Persephone wanted to tell him. *This is Mount Olympus Academy. Nothing bad will happen here.*

"Eeee!" a girl's voice screamed at a deafening pitch. Persephone cringed as Atë and several of her friends raced down the school's granite steps to the courtyard. "I can't believe they're here!" Atë continued in a voice made unnaturally screechy by excitement.

Orpheus and Eurydice hopped out of the chariot, and the tattooed bodyguard leaped down beside them. Viper reached into the chariot for the visitors' luggage just in the nick of time. Because, already, Hermes had begun lifting off again.

Typical, thought Persephone. *Hermes could certainly be unmannerly when he was in a hurry. Which he usually was.*

She looked around. Atë and her friends were still staring at the newcomers, wearing stunned, starstruck expressions. This was no way to treat guests.

Persephone stepped forward. "Welcome to Mount Olympus Academy," she told the two stars and their bodyguard politely. "Are you here to see Principal Zeus?" She hoped they hadn't come without asking permission, because Zeus didn't deal kindly with uninvited guests. Of course, Hermes probably wouldn't have brought them if Zeus hadn't already approved their visit.

Before any of the visitors could reply, a boy somewhere behind her shouted, "Orpheus! You're early!" She turned to see Apollo running down the Academy's front steps. He raced across the courtyard, heading their way.

As Apollo skidded to a halt before them, Viper stepped in front of Orpheus and Eurydice. Did he think Apollo was going to attack them or something? Talk about overprotective! He was worse than her mom was at times.

"We'll need accommodations," the bodyguard told Apollo curtly.

"Sure. We'll figure all that out," Apollo assured him.

"Orpheus and you can stay in the boys' dorm, and Eurydice in the girls'."

More students came along now, including Dionysus and Ares. They joined the others clustered around Orpheus. A hand touched Persephone's. She turned her head to see that Eurydice had slipped over to stand beside her. The girl gestured to the autograph on Persephone's arm.

"I remember you," said Eurydice. "You're that flower girl from the concert." She raised her voice. "Look, Orpheus. The flower girl's still got your autograph."

"Cool," said Orpheus.

Persephone folded her arms across her middle so the autograph wouldn't show. She had been careful not to wash it off, wanting it to last as long as possible after the concert. Now she was a little embarrassed. She hoped Orpheus and Eurydice wouldn't think she hadn't bathed since Saturday night!

As Apollo, Orpheus, Viper, and the other guys discussed visiting arrangements, Eurydice linked arms with Persephone. "Want to hang out?" the pink-haired girl asked.

"Um, well, sure," Persephone replied, feeling surprised and flattered. "I still have one more class to go to today, though."

"How fun!" Eurydice bounced on her toes in excitement. "I'll come with you. Maybe we can even be roomies while I'm here, huh? I mean, I felt like we connected when you were onstage, you know? It's like I've known you practically all my life!"

Persephone had no idea she'd felt that way. It was kind of strange, since their meeting had been so brief, but it was nice, too. "I don't room in the dorms. I live at home with my mom," she admitted.

Eurydice blinked at her, looking disappointed.

"It's p-pretty. Our garden is awesome," Persephone stammered. She felt like her status with this girl was wilting, like some of those early flowers she'd cultivated for the Underworld. "My mom created these magical daffodils that sing in our garden. And I taught them to perform one of the duets that you and Orpheus do!"

"How mega-riffic!" said Eurydice, brightening again. "I have posilutely absotively *got* to see them sing that song or I'll just die! How about if I spend the night at your house tonight? We can hang out and do girl stuff. Sound fun?"

An amazing pop star wanted to stay over at her house? The old, *dependable* Persephone might have hesitated at least half a second, but the *daring* Persephone rushed to agree before the girl changed her mind. "Okay. Sure!"

Ping! Ping! The lyrebell rang out signaling that fifth

period was about to begin. Everyone moved toward the Academy's front doors.

"Orpheus and Viper can come with me to Music-ology class, since you and Ares have that test in Revenge-ology," Persephone overheard Dionysus say to Apollo. Then Dionysus looked over at Eurydice.

"She's with me," Persephone said quickly. "We're going to Spell-ology."

As it turned out, Ms. Hecate, the Spell-ology teacher, was giving a review on elixirs and potions. However, the only person really paying attention was Athena, who was the brainiest student at MOA. For Persephone and everyone else, class was pretty much a blur. They were all too excited about having a star in their midst.

After class Persephone gave Eurydice a brief tour of the Academy, ending up in the cafeteria. By now everyone was buzzing with excitement about their rock star guests.

It seemed to Persephone that the whole cafeteria turned to stare when they walked in. She felt like there was a spotlight shining on her as she took Eurydice to the dinner line. But Eurydice seemed unfazed. She just smiled, said hi to everyone, kept up a constant stream of chatter, and gave autographs when she was asked.

Seeing Hades up ahead in the dinner line, Persephone waved to him. He sent her a smile in return.

"Who's that?" asked Eurydice.

"Hades," Persephone replied easily. "Godboy of the Underworld."

"Ooh! He's kee-*yute*!" said Eurydice.

Persephone smiled at her enthusiasm. He was more handsome than cute in her opinion, but she didn't say so.

When the eight-armed cafeteria lady offered the girls the ambrosia surprise for dinner, Persephone elbowed Eurydice and gave her head a little shake. It was the one dish at school that most students agreed wasn't very good. They both reached for plates of nectaroni with a side of yambrosia instead.

After they got their trays, Eurydice scanned the cafeteria with her gaze. "You'll sit with me, right?" she asked, sounding kind of shy.

"Of course," said Persephone, steering her toward the table where she always sat with her three best friends. Like her, she knew they'd be thrilled to have Eurydice at their table.

Suddenly a bright smile filled Eurydice's face. "There's Orpheus and your friend Hades." Swerving, she headed off in the direction of the godboys' table.

"Wait!" said Persephone, hurrying after her. "You're going to sit with the *guys*?"

Eurydice flicked her head, flipping her pink hair over one shoulder. "Sure, why not?"

101

"Well, I usually sit with my goddessgirl friends," said Persephone.

"Boys in one place. Girls in another." Eurydice sang the words as if they were a song. "Don't you think it's dull to do the same old thing? Let's shake it up a little. Be free spirits. I mean, who wants to be boring and sit in the same place with the same people all the time?"

Persephone stiffened. "Boring" made her think of "dependable," which was exactly what she did not want to be. She'd tried a new style for the concert Friday night, and that had gone well, so . . . "Yeah. Okay, let's do it," she said.

As they headed for the boys' table, she glanced over her shoulder at her usual table. Athena and Aphrodite were there, but Artemis hadn't arrived yet. She sent her two friends an apologetic look. Then she followed Eurydice.

Persephone really liked sitting with her goddess-girl friends. Still, she had often wondered what god-boys talked about at their table. This was her chance to find out!

7

Daisies

Persephone

UNFORTUNATELY, THE BOYS WERE TOO BUSY peppering Orpheus and Eurydice with questions about their music and what it was like to be rock stars to talk about whatever they usually talked about. Hades, who was sitting across from Persephone, was mostly quiet. She could tell he was taking everything in, though.

After a while some of the boys started acting goofy,

building stuff out of food on their plates, then blowing it up. *Huh?* Were they doing this for her and Eurydice's benefit? Did they really think girls were *impressed* by that sort of behavior? Hades noticed her watching the other guys, and the two of them shared a grin. Apparently he thought his friends were acting goofy too.

When dinner was over, Persephone took both her and Eurydice's trays to the tray return. By then her three best friends had already finished dinner and were gone. She ran into Hades on the way back to his table.

"Want to hang out for a while before you head home?" he asked her.

She shook her head. "Can't. Not today."

"Oh," Hades said, sounding disappointed. "You've got something else going on?"

"I'm taking Eurydice home with me." She'd been planning to make a quick trip to the Underworld before it got dark, to plant his birthday flower. Looked like that would have to be put on hold now that Eurydice would be spending the night.

Hades arched an eyebrow. "So you guys are friends now?"

"Sort of. She asked to sleep over, and I thought it would be fun. Is there something you want to talk about?" Persephone asked. When he said nothing right away, she went on. "I could stay, but not too long. Because the trip home will probably be slower than normal since Eurydice isn't used to flying by winged sandal. And Mom doesn't like me flying after dark, as you know."

Hades still didn't say anything, but from the way he shifted his shoulders, she could tell he didn't exactly approve.

"What's wrong? Don't you like Eurydice? I do," said Persephone.

"I don't really know her," Hades said. "But she seems kind of flighty."

"Flighty? What does that even mean?"

"It means she likes to follow her whims without giving them much forethought. And that could lead her—and maybe you—into trouble."

Persephone's jaw dropped at the injustice of his comment. "What? No, she doesn't! What makes you say that?"

Hades nodded toward Eurydice, who was now standing on a chair demonstrating a dance move for some of the other girls. When she executed a spin on one tiptoe, her sandal slipped. She started to topple off the chair. Persephone and Hades both instinctively took a step in her direction, though they were much too far away to help.

Luckily Viper was nearby and saved her, catching her in his arms and setting her back on the ground. Eurydice laughed, not seeming to realize there could have been awful consequences to her actions if she'd fallen. Bruises at the very least!

"Well, it's only for one night. And I promise we won't dance on any chairs," Persephone told Hades wryly. This managed to wring a rare smile from him. "Anyway, what did you want to talk about?"

An earnest look came into his eyes. "Well, it's about that poll in the—"

"Persephone!" Eurydice squealed, then dashed over to join her. "Ready to go? I can hardly wait to see your place." Then she glanced at Hades in surprise. "Oh. Sorry. Did I interrupt something?"

Hades shoved his hands into the pockets of his tunic. "S'okay," he said. "No big deal."

But Persephone had a feeling that whatever he wanted to say about the poll was more important than he was letting on. Before she could question him about it further, Ares and Apollo wandered over.

"Can we count on you to sit in with the band again tonight?" Apollo asked Hades. "Word from Principal Zeus is that Poseidon will be gone till next week investigating that shipwreck."

As the boys began discussing their band practice, Persephone waved to Hades. Catching his eye, she mouthed a good-bye as she and Eurydice left the cafeteria. They made a couple of quick stops so Persephone could get her scrollbag and Eurydice could grab her small overnight bag.

Heads turned and excited whispers followed in their wake as they walked side by side down the hall toward the enormous bronze front doors of the Academy. Persephone felt cooler than cool that this rock star had chosen *her* to hang out with.

"Wait," she told Eurydice when they reached the

doors. "We'll need winged sandals." Both girls dropped their bags onto the floor. *Plop, plop!*

Bracing a hand on the wall, Persephone slipped off her sandals. She set them neatly on the floor by the wall and then grabbed two pairs of winged ones from a big basket. She handed one pair to Eurydice.

"I'm guessing you've never flown before?" she asked Eurydice, who was slipping off her own sandals.

Eurydice's eyes sparkled. "No, but I absotively adore trying new things."

"Me too," said Persephone. "Lately anyway."

As soon as they stepped outside together, they hung their bags over their shoulders and put their traveling sandals on. The sandals' straps immediately twined around their ankles. The silver wings at Persephone's heels began to flap.

Eurydice stared down at her feet. "Why aren't my wings moving?"

"They don't work for mortals," Persephone explained. "Unless you're holding the hand of an immortal." She reached out and took the other girl's hand. Immediately the wings on Eurydice's sandals began to flap.

Persephone leaned forward slightly, and Eurydice copied her. Their sandals whisked them away! Together they skimmed down Mount Olympus, passing through a ring of clouds as they sailed toward Earth.

Eurydice quickly got the hang of winged travel. "This is posilutely wing-tastic!" she said, leaning this way and that.

Most mortals were so nervous on their first flights that they teetered off balance, but she didn't seem nervous at all as they sped along. In fact, her daring was making *Persephone* kind of nervous.

Besides leaning one way and then another, Eurydice sometimes bent her knees until she was almost sitting.

She even did a little dance step now and then in midair that caused them to wobble midflight. She wasn't just daring, Persephone decided. Eurydice was a dare*devil*.

"Careful," Persephone murmured more than once.

The wind whistled in their ears as they whipped past boulders and trees. Suddenly a lock of Eurydice's long pink hair blew across her face. Automatically she pulled her hand away from Persephone's, to smooth the hair back out of her eyes. And just like that, the girl was falling.

"No!" yelled Persephone. Dipping low, she managed to grab Eurydice's hand in the nick of time.

"Woo-hoo! What fun!" said Eurydice. She laughed as she adjusted the straps of her bag on her shoulder with one hand, seemingly oblivious to her near-disaster.

Persephone's heart, however, was thumping wildly. "Don't do that again," she warned. Didn't this girl realize she could have been seriously hurt?

Eurydice gently bumped her shoulder against Persephone's. "Oh, lighten up," she said in a teasing tone. "I'm okay. And don't worry. I won't tell anyone you nearly lost me."

Persephone's eyes widened at the unfairness of that statement. Eurydice had let go of *her* hand. Not the other way around.

By the time they reached Persephone's house, it was nearly dark. *Mew! Mew!* A black-and-white kitten scampered out to greet them.

Eurydice picked him up. "Who's this little cutie?"

Persephone smiled. "His name's Adonis. Isn't it, little sweetie-weetie?" she cooed. She stroked his sleek fur. He started purring immediately.

"Aphrodite and I share him," she told Eurydice. "He's mine this week. Next week he's hers. Then mine again."

In the kitchen Persephone found a note and showed

it to Eurydice. "It's from my mom. She's working late tonight in her flower shop in the Immortal Marketplace." After they got a simple snack and fed Adonis, they went into Persephone's room.

"Nice poster," Eurydice commented, grinning at the poster on Persephone's wall of Orpheus rocking out. It was next to a drawing of Hades winning the long jump competition during the Olympic Games. She'd gotten both from *Teen Scrollazine*.

Persephone grinned back. "Thanks." She liked decorating. Her room had a daisy theme. Her throw rug was shaped like a daisy, and so was her mirror. Even the Orpheus poster and the picture of Hades were edged in frames with daisy designs.

Eurydice pointed to a box of loose silk daisies on the floor in a corner of Persephone's room. "What are those for?"

"I was thinking of using them to make a divider curtain between my desk and the rest of the room," Persephone explained. "But I haven't gotten around to it. I was going to tie the daisies about every ten inches on long strings that would reach from the ceiling to the floor. You'd be able to see through them like with a beaded curtain, but they'd still visually divide the space in my room."

"I *love* that idea!" said Eurydice. "Got any string?"

"You mean you want to help me string the daisies? Now?"

Eurydice nodded enthusiastically. "Sure, why not?"

"Okay," said Persephone. "Thanks!" She did have homework, but nothing that couldn't wait till tomorrow night.

They'd only strung a few strands of the daisy curtain, though, when Eurydice got an idea for a different room arrangement that she wanted to try. They moved Persephone's bed at an angle. But that also meant they then needed to move the dresser, the rug, a chair, and some other random stuff.

Adonis had curled into a ball and fallen asleep at the end of Persephone's bed. He didn't twitch a whisker when they moved it. Noise and people running around never bothered him a bit. In fact, the more noise, the happier he was. He was the best, cutest kitten ever!

After they moved the furniture, the two girls stayed up late chatting, sharing ambrosia chips and dip, and laughing about silly stuff. Persephone told her new friend about the Truth or Dare game that had led to her asking Orpheus for his autograph.

And Eurydice told *her* about life as a pop star, and that she'd first met Orpheus in second grade! So then Persephone told her about the first time she'd really talked with Hades. (In a cemetery!) And about how her friends had thought he was bad news at first.

Eurydice was easy to talk to. She also had amazing decorating ideas. Ideas that kept them busy till Persephone's mom got home around ten.

"Oh, Persy, I'm having so much fun!" exclaimed Eurydice as they were putting on their pj's. "You know what? I should stay all week. Then we could get your whole room fixed up cute. I have a lot of ideas, but I travel so much with the band that I don't have time to decorate my *own* room. What do you say?"

This megastar girl wanted to spend every night this week at her house? And help decorate her room?

"I say yes!" said Persephone.

Eurydice reached out and gave her a quick hug. "It's like we're best friends after just a few hours of hanging out!"

"Yeah!" Persephone agreed. Eurydice had even given her a special nickname—Persy—as if they really were BFFs. Hades was wrong about this girl. She was super-nice. And it was going to be fun to hang out with her all week long.

The next morning, however, Persephone frowned at her room as she got ready for school. In all the excitement of being with Eurydice last night, she hadn't realized how much had been left undone.

Half-started decorating projects and strewn daisies were everywhere. And she wasn't so sure she really liked the new furniture arrangement after all. Plus, they'd completely forgotten to listen to the garden flowers singing that duet!

It was only Tuesday though. Eurydice would be here the rest of the week, so they could hear the song some other afternoon. And they could discuss the redecorating in the following days as well. She only hoped her mom wouldn't look in her room anytime soon. It was a wreck!

After digging around in her scrollbag, Persephone pulled out a papyrus pass she'd gotten the day before from Ms. Hydra, Zeus's nine-headed administrative assistant.

"What's that?" asked Eurydice as she grabbed her own small bag.

"An Underworld pass. I need to go down there some-time today for a Garden-ology class project I'm doing. The project is kind of a secret, though."

"Oh! A secret project? Do tell," said Eurydice.

"Hades' birthday is next Saturday," said Persephone. "I've got a surprise planned, that's all."

"It's silly for you to go out of your way. Just take me with you and we'll head there now. Then we can go on to MOA together afterward."

Persephone considered this idea. It would save time to go to the Underworld now instead of later. "Okay," she said. "But you'll have to wait for me on the banks of the River Styx. Mortals can't enter the Underworld. It's against the rules."

"Rules schmules," said Eurydice.

Persephone gave her what she hoped was a stern look. "I'm not kidding."

"Oh, all right. I'll wait. I don't mind," said Eurydice. "Actually I'd love a peek at the Underworld, even if it's only from the outside. Inspiration for my songwriting, you know?"

"Speaking of songs, what about Orpheus?" said Persephone, just remembering him. "Should we let him know you're going to be late to MOA?"

Eurydice shrugged. "Oh, yeah. I forgot we have a band practice planned. But he won't mind if I don't show."

Persephone wasn't so sure. Not wanting Orpheus to worry, she quickly summoned a magic breeze so the girls could send a message to him at MOA. Turned out that Eurydice hadn't even told him she was spending the night with Persephone! In the message the girls explained that they'd be late, and that Eurydice planned to stay the nights with Persephone all week.

After the breeze took the message away, the two girls put on their winged sandals so they could fly. And then they were off to the Underworld!

8

Roommates

Hades

KNOCK. KNOCK. KNOCK.

Hades opened his dorm room door at eight o'clock on Monday night to see Orpheus standing in the hall, his hand raised to knock again.

"Hey, dude," Orpheus said in greeting.

Hades stood back in surprise as the rock star casually walked past him, coming inside without being invited.

"Uh, yeah, hey," said Hades, not moving from the doorway. "Can I help you with something?"

"Oh, sure, bring in my bags. Thanks." He'd left his two overnight bags sitting in the dorm hall just outside Hades' door.

Hades folded his arms, waiting and not saying a word. It was a technique he often used on misbehaving shades in the Underworld. It made them nervous and quickly got them to explain themselves. It worked on Orpheus now too.

"Heracles said your roommate is gone," Orpheus told him. He was walking all around the small room, taking it all in. "Okay if I bunk with you for the week?"

Hades frowned. "Me? Why? I mean, where's Viper?" He looked up and down the hall, hoping to spot the tattooed bodyguard so he'd come take this megastar guy off his hands.

"Viper's rooming with Heracles. They bonded over discussions of weaponry and feats of strength. Hardly even noticed when I left." Orpheus grinned.

Hades couldn't help grinning a little in return. "Well—," he began uncertainly.

"And the truth is," Orpheus went on, "I think the Underworld would be a fascinating subject for a song. I'd like the inside scoop. And the word is, you're the guy who knows all about that place."

He was peering at a map of the Underworld on Hades' bulletin board now. Across the room Poseidon's bulletin board had maps of various seas.

Hades' brows rose. "Oh, well, okay I guess. But if you do write a song about it, be sure to warn mortals they aren't welcome there." He'd managed to calm the Furies the other night, but they'd be riled up again if more mortals came lurking around the Underworld.

Since Orpheus's bags were still in the hall, Hades lugged them in and dropped them by Poseidon's bed.

"Careful! My lyre's in there," said Orpheus. "It's one of a kind." He ran to the bag, pulled his twelve-string lyre out, and carefully inspected it.

Hades glanced toward his desk. He'd been catching up on some homework, but he supposed he could abandon it to hang out with his unexpected guest. Only, he wasn't sure what to do to entertain a rock star.

Suddenly Orpheus cocked his head, listening intently. "Is that music I hear?"

Hades nodded. "Some of the guys are jamming in the common room at the end of the hall. And I just remembered I promised to stand in on drums while Poseidon's away. Want to go?" he asked hopefully.

Orpheus was already heading out the door with his lyre.

"I'll take that as a yes," Hades said to his empty room. Grinning slightly, he followed.

Down in the common room Apollo, Dionysus, and Ares were warming up. They welcomed Orpheus and Hades.

"Apollo says you're on drums tonight?" Ares asked Hades.

"Yeah, so hold on to your ears," Hades warned jokingly.

He was actually pretty good on drums. Apollo had asked him to join Heavens Above way back when the band had first formed, but he'd been too busy in the Underworld. Besides that, he didn't like being the center of attention onstage. So Poseidon had become the band's drummer instead. Hades liked sitting in for practices and jam sessions like this now and then, though.

Once the first note sounded, the time flew by. With

Orpheus singing and playing, the band sounded even more amazing than usual. Almost magical.

"It's getting hot," Orpheus noted after a while. "Can you open the windows wider?"

"Wimp," Ares teased. "Ask Hades if you want to know what heat really is."

Orpheus grinned. "I plan to. I'm hoping he'll give me some inside info about the Underworld for a song Eurydice and I are writing."

"First thing you need to know is that the Underworld is waaay hotter than this. At least near the lava pits," Hades informed him. Since he was closest to the windows, he got up to fling them wide open.

"Whoa!" Hades said, taken aback by the sight that met his eyes. "Guys! Come look at this! I think Orpheus has got some new fans."

Outside, a variety of night creatures had gathered.

Wombats, raccoons, ocelots, leopards, foxes, and more. They were all over the place. Curled up on the marble benches, crouched down in the flowerbeds, lying around on the tiled courtyard floor. Nightingales and owls lined the Academy's windowsills to listen too. Bats filled the sky, swooping and darting gracefully.

"Wow! This has never happened before," said Apollo. He and the others had joined Hades at the window and were surveying the scene in amazement.

"It's Orpheus's music," said Dionysus. "It's got to be. It must've enchanted them into coming out of the forest to listen!"

Orpheus smiled and shrugged, glancing at the animals. "No biggie. This kind of stuff happens to me all the time."

Suddenly footsteps came pounding down the hall. They got louder and louder. Closer and closer. The boys turned to look just as the door to the common room flew open. It banged the wall so hard that one of the hinges broke.

Principal Zeus stood in the doorway. All seven fierce feet of him! His eyes were blazing as they searched every face in the room. Slowly he raised a muscled arm and pointed an accusing finger in their direction. Sparks of electricity snapped and sizzled along his arm. Was he about to blast them all to smithereens for playing their music too loudly on a school night?

The principal opened his mouth to speak. The boys held their breath. Then he smiled. Big. An expression of bliss came over his face.

"Why'd you stop playing that *captivating* music?" he demanded in a bemused voice.

The godboys gaped at him. It seemed no one was immune to the power of Orpheus's musical skills. Even Zeus—the King of the Gods and Ruler of the Heavens, not to mention principal of MOA—was a fan.

9

Planting Deeds

Persephone

As Eurydice and Persephone neared the shore of the River Styx opposite from the Underworld side Tuesday morning, they saw a group of girls hanging around there.

"Who are *they*?" Eurydice wondered aloud.

"Good question," said Persephone. She could tell they were mortal right away because their skin didn't shimmer. But what were they doing here?

She dipped lower and read one of the signs they held.

WE ♥ HADES! *Huh?*

"Looks like your crush has a fan club," said Eurydice. "Awesome! Now I'll have some friends to hang out with while you're off gardening. I kind of hate being alone."

Persephone glanced at her in surprise. She would've thought everyone needed alone time now and then to think and just, well, be alone. Rock stars must be different, though. They were probably used to lots of fans hanging around.

The two girls touched down near the ferry dock. Persephone immediately bent and wrapped her sandals' laces around the wings to keep them from flapping, so she could walk at normal speed. Of course, Eurydice didn't have to do anything with her laces. Her wings had stopped flapping the minute Persephone had let go of her hand.

The ferryboat was already coming toward them, having just dropped a load of passengers in the Underworld. A grizzled, stooped man was at the helm. Captain Charon. Persephone waved to him, and he tooted his horn in greeting.

One of the mortal girls squealed in excitement when she suddenly noticed the two girls. "It's Persephone! And Eurydice!" she shouted.

Persephone clutched her scrollbag and backed away, a little startled as the girls ran toward them. However, Eurydice dropped her bag and spread her arms wide in greeting. "Hi, everyone!" she shouted gleefully.

"Need a ride to the Underworld?" Charon inquired as his ferry docked.

"Yes, please," Persephone called to him.

"Will you be okay?" she asked Eurydice before heading for the boat. "I'll be back as soon as—"

"Go ahead. I'm fine here," Eurydice interrupted, waving her away. She'd already begun to sign autographs, seeming delighted by all the attention.

"All right, then. Back in a few," said Persephone. She dashed over and stepped onto the ferryboat just as it was about to leave again. A dozen or so shades—souls of the dead—had already boarded.

"What brings you down here this morning?" Charon asked her. His mournful voice always reminded her of a foghorn.

She smiled. She'd been to visit the Underworld so many times that she and Charon were friends now. She held up her scrollbag and shook it so the box of hybrid seeds inside rattled intriguingly.

"I've brought a surprise. For Hades' birthday. But I

can't tell you any more than that," she said.

"Glad you're doing something special for that boy," Charon replied. "He likes you. I can tell. Wears that amulet you gave him everywhere."

"What amulet?" Persephone asked blankly. She'd never given Hades such a gift.

"The one with the seed in it," Charon said matter-of-factly, which only made Persephone more curious.

"What kind of seed?" she asked.

But Charon didn't answer. His attention was divided between steering the boat and counting the silver coins in the old burlap bag he kept tied to his belt. All the shades paid him one obol as their fare to ride the ferry into the Underworld.

Finished with his counting, he concentrated on guiding the boat toward the far shore. Apparently having forgotten her question, he said, "Hades has been stressed out lately. It's all these mortal fans. They've been trying to sneak into the Underworld ever since he went and got his name on some list in."

"You mean the *Teen Scrollazine* poll?" Persephone asked. That was what Hades had wanted to talk about yesterday when he'd stopped her in the cafeteria after dinner! Had he wanted her advice on how to handle these fangirls?

Charon nodded. "Yeah, a poll—that's it. Caused this whole problem." As the river branched into a swamp, his brow furrowed. It took all his skill to get his boat safely to the opposite side of the river.

Although Persephone was mega-curious about the amulet seed he'd mentioned, she didn't want to bother him and cause a wreck!

When the ferry finally bumped against the shore, she tried again. "Charon? About that amulet—"

But now he was busy docking. "Underworld station! Everybody off!" he called out.

There was some grumbling among the shades as they began leaving the boat. Persephone was swept along with the crowd and could only wave farewell to Charon now. She soon managed to separate herself from the shades as they filed past Cerberus, Hades' enormous guard dog with three slobbering heads. When he let out a roar, gasps rippled over the crowd, and they drew back in fear.

Persephone wasn't worried. Because, despite his appearance, Cerberus was actually a big softie. After giving him a pat on each of his heads, she slipped past the shades, who were now lining up to be judged by two of Hades' helpers.

A gray mist swirled around her ankles as she set off across a wide field. Parts of the Underworld—like this field—weren't hot at all. In fact the surrounding mist felt refreshingly cool. Although she liked the sunshine and blue skies of Mount Olympus, she also liked it here in the Underworld, where it was peaceful and shadowy. She could never quite decide which place she preferred.

When the ground turned muddy, Persephone unleashed the silver wings on her sandals. The wings began to flap, and soon she was skimming several inches above the gloomy swamp.

In the distance she could see a high green hedge. Beyond it were the Elysian Fields—the Underworld's most desirable neighborhood. The dead who were lucky enough to go there feasted, played, and sang forever more.

But she wouldn't plant her special hybrid seeds in that place. It was already beautiful with fruit trees and meadows. Trouble rarely visited the Elysian Fields, so Hades rarely visited it either. She wanted her flowers to grow in a place where he would see them almost every day.

A few minutes later she reached her destination, a small castle built of black stone. This was Hades' home when he wasn't at MOA.

"Godness! So this is the infamous castle," she murmured. She'd never seen it till now, but Hades had told her all about it. He'd called it forlorn.

Talk about an understatement! Dark mist swirled around the castle, and a swampy moat surrounded it. A gloomdial (which worked sort of like a sundial to tell time) stood in the yard near the drawbridge. From the outside the castle looked abandoned, lonely, and almost . . . creepy.

Far beyond it was Tartarus, which Persephone *had* seen. It was the worst place in the Underworld, where the truly evil wound up—including those who had offended the gods and goddesses. Not a very welcoming place at all!

She knew the Underworld wasn't supposed to be like an amusement park or anything. But that didn't mean it had to be *totally* gloomy! So she was going to do what she could to brighten things up for Hades around here.

She took the box full of hybrid seeds from her scroll-bag and opened it. Then she chanted a quick spell:

"Prepare yourself, soil,
For these seeds I'll sow.
Become a rich bed,
Where flowers will grow!"

Instantly the moat drained and the ground on either side of the castle drawbridge raked itself up into two beds of fertile soil.

When all was ready, Persephone worked fast, dropping

the seeds about ten inches apart in the freshly tilled sections of dirt. As soon as a seed fell from her fingers, the nearby soil magically covered it up.

Now and then she checked over her shoulder. Since Hades often had to leave school to check on things here, he could appear in the Underworld at any time. Her fingers were crossed that he wouldn't catch her and ruin the surprise.

Finally her box was empty. She chanted a "good timing" spell that would cause all the flowers to bloom exactly at noon on Hades' birthday.

> *"On Saturday noon,*
> *Flowers, please bloom!*
> *To brighten this castle*
> *And banish the gloom."*

Then she recited one last spell—a "hiding" one. It would keep this newly tilled garden invisible until she was ready to show it to Hades.

A peek at the gloomdial told her the planting had taken longer than expected. Her Underworld pass was only good for one class period and would expire the minute second period began. She needed to hurry!

Hades would not have approved if he'd known what she *dared* to do next. Which was to take a shortcut back to the ferry dock. One that went through the Forbidden Meadow.

As she zipped along in her winged sandals, colorful, hissing snakes slithered among the grasses of the meadow below her. *Ssss! Ssss!*

"Ye gods!" Persephone muttered warily. Hades had told her the snakes were extremely poisonous. Of course, they couldn't touch her as long as she was careful to stay high above them and out of reach. Still, taking this shortcut hadn't been one of her best ideas.

She made it through the meadow without mishap and breathed a sigh of relief. On her return ferryboat trip, Charon was busy repairing a small leak he'd just found and was in no mood for chatting. Upon reaching the other side of the River Styx, she found Eurydice entertaining the mortal girls with a story about her life.

"Being a pop star is *amaaazingly* fun," she was saying. "For me it's all about having a passion for fashion, signing autographs, and most of all making music. And just think—six months ago I wasn't a star. I was just like you. So if you have a dream, you *can* make it happen!"

The girls were hanging on her every word. Even though she was a mortal and couldn't perform real magic, Eurydice certainly had a magical personality, thought

Persephone. Orpheus did too. They had star power!

As the two girls headed back to MOA, Eurydice was full of questions about the Underworld. Persephone told her what she knew, describing the places she'd seen. The fabulously beautiful Elysian Fields, the frightening Forbidden Meadow, and terrifying Tartarus with its rivers of lava, just to name a few.

Soon their feet touched down in the Academy courtyard. Seeing Aphrodite on the steps leading up to the front doors, the two girls hurried to join her.

"Where'd you get that awesome chiton?" Eurydice asked her. Persephone had been silently admiring it too. It was a gorgeous new lacy pink chiton she hadn't seen before.

"The Immortal Marketplace," said Aphrodite. Grinning, she struck a fashion model pose, one hand on her hip and the other fluffing her hair.

"Ooh! I've heard about that place," said Eurydice.

As they approached the doors of the Academy, she fell into step with Aphrodite, forcing Persephone to walk behind since there wasn't room for all three of them to go through the doors together.

"It's where goddesses and gods shop, right?" Eurydice went on as they walked inside. Caught up in her excitement, she let the heavy bronze front door go. It almost shut in Persephone's face! Would have too if Persephone hadn't caught it in time and pushed it wide so she could go through.

"I'd love to see it," Eurydice was saying to Aphrodite. "Maybe we should go shopping there after school?"

"Sure," Aphrodite replied easily. "I'm always up for shopping."

"Me too! Maybe I could even sleep over tonight?" Eurydice suggested. "Persephone said you have a spare bed in your dorm room, right? We could look through your closets. Maybe do a little mixing and matching. Talk fashion queen to fashion queen. What do you say?"

Catching up to the other two girls, Persephone glanced at Eurydice in dismay. Had she already forgotten their plans? The decorating? The hanging out they were going to do at her house?

At least Aphrodite hadn't forgotten. "But Ares told me Orpheus got a message this morning that you'd be staying at Persephone's every night this week," she told Eurydice uncertainly.

"Oh, it was nothing definite. She won't mind," Eurydice said carelessly. She turned toward Persephone. "Will you, Persy?"

"N-no," said Persephone, even though she *did* mind. Truth was, she felt totally slighted. Until now she'd thought Eurydice had specifically singled *her* out to befriend. Wrong!

Persephone could feel her smile trembling. She wanted to say how she *really* felt. But she wasn't like the confident Medusa, who could just blurt out her feelings about anything and everything.

Still, Aphrodite must've sensed her disappointment. "Persephone, you should stay over too," she suggested. "Why don't you bunk with Artemis tonight so we can all do things together?"

Eurydice squealed in delight and gave Persephone a hug. "Yes, you have to stay, Persy. You just have to," she urged. "It wouldn't be nearly as fun without you."

And just like that, Persephone felt wanted and dazzled all over again. So dazzled that for a minute she forgot about Artemis's three slobbery dogs. Unlike Aphrodite, Persephone didn't really mind them, though. She'd deal. And she didn't want to miss all the fun. Amazing rock stars didn't visit MOA every day, after all!

"What's your next class?" Eurydice asked Persephone when the lyrebell rang to signal the end of first period. Students soon began pouring out of classes into the hall.

"Beast-ology," Persephone replied, just as Athena came over to join them. "We're doing in-class reports on recent magical beast sightings from Earth."

"Sounds awesome!" said Eurydice.

"Didn't you hear?" asked Athena. "My dad's canceled all second- and third-period classes. Instead there's going to be a concert in the courtyard so everyone can hear our musical guests perform."

"Turns out that Principal Zeus is a total fan of Orpheus's," Aphrodite added.

"And of me too, I hope," Eurydice said. She sounded a little miffed at not being mentioned.

"I'm sure he will be," Athena said politely, "when he hears you perform."

Eurydice perked up. "Now's my chance to wow him, then! Once you've performed for the King of the Gods and Ruler of the Heavens, you've pretty much made it to the big time, right? After the concert I'll have to send a press release to *Teen Scrollazine* to let my fans know."

"I can help with that," Pheme chimed in. She'd been lurking just outside their circle, listening in.

"Perfect! Thanks!" said Eurydice. After saying good-bye, she hurried down to join the band, which was beginning to set up in the courtyard.

Students quickly found seats on benches or set out blankets to sit on, spreading them around the make-shift stage. Persephone and Athena perched on a high stone wall, where they'd have a good view. Artemis and Aphrodite sat on a marble bench nearby.

Eurydice and Orpheus were huddled together talking near the stage now. The band was warming up.

Seeing that Hades was helping set up their equipment, Persephone waved to him, and he grinned back.

Minutes later Orpheus climbed onstage to thunderous applause. Eurydice joined him along with Heavens Above members Ares, Dionysus, and Apollo. Hades moved to the back of the stage, to sit in for Poseidon on drums.

For the first number, Orpheus played and sang a solo tune. His voice and lyre rang throughout the courtyard. One by one, animals from the nearby forest drew closer, entranced by the music. Squirrels scampered up to the benches. Rabbits hopped over to sit in the flowerbeds. Ducks waddled near. Even Artemis's golden-horned deer came to listen.

Soon cute furry creatures ringed the students in the courtyard. Birds of every color filled the trees. Even butterflies fluttered in to rest gently on bushes and on MOA's rooftop.

Up in his office Zeus flung open the windows overlooking the courtyard so that he and Ms. Hydra could listen too. As she leaned out the window, all nine of Ms. Hydra's heads were smiling—even her grumpy green head. Orpheus's music was just that good!

The band joined in on the second song. Orpheus sang lead, and Eurydice sang backup. Just like last Saturday's concert, their harmony was amazing.

After several more songs Orpheus made an announcement. "Eurydice and I would now like to perform something brand-new! I wrote the tune some time ago, but she wrote the lyrics just this morning. Our song is called 'Truth or Dare'!"

What? Persephone straightened in surprise.

As the song began, she realized that Eurydice had used the things Persephone had told her, to help inspire this new song. Like about the autograph dare and her first meeting with Hades. It wasn't like that stuff was secret or anything. But she sort of felt betrayed that Eurydice hadn't asked first if she could use the information in this public way.

She had to admit that the song was good, though: "I dare you, dare you, daaare you to talk to the bad-news boy, boy, boy . . ."

At the end of the song, Eurydice tossed out dares to people in the crowd. They were silly things that made people laugh. She dared Ares to do a cartwheel. He did it, then took a bow. Iris was dared to create a rainbow in the shape of a heart in the sky. She did, and it was beautiful.

But when Eurydice dared Medusa to make her snakes do a hula dance, Medusa refused.

There was an awkward pause. Then Eurydice turned to Hades, who was at the back of the stage.

"Okay, let's dare Hades to do something instead. Hmm. What should it be? Persephone, got any ideas?"

Everyone turned to look at Persephone. She squirmed, not knowing what to say.

Eurydice laughed. "Come on. Let's dare him to do something out of his comfort zone. I know! A little bird told me he's mega-talented on those drums. So . . ." She looked directly at Hades. "I dare you to perform a drum solo!"

Though Hades didn't like being the center of attention any more than Persephone did, he was a good sport about it. Grinning slightly, he tossed his drumsticks into the air, caught them, and played a short but dramatic solo.

Athena leaned over to Persephone. "Wow! He's great!"

Persephone nodded. Athena was right. He was every

bit as good on drums as Poseidon. Maybe better!

Hades' solo led into the next song, and the performance continued smoothly, tune after tune. As Persephone watched him, she could tell he was having fun. Still, she wished Eurydice hadn't dared him right in front of everyone like that. Afterward, when students were heading inside for lunch, she went to the back of the stage to explain things to him.

"I can't believe you told Eurydice all that stuff for her song!" he exclaimed before she could say a word. "I really don't appreciate being put on the spot. Or in the spotlight. You know how I feel about that."

Whoa! He might not have acted upset onstage, but he certainly sounded like he was now.

"Yeah, about that," Persephone began. "I didn't know she would—"

Cutting her short, Hades said, "I've got enough

to worry about right now because of that dumb *Teen Scrollazine* poll." He stood and began packing up the drum set.

"It wasn't so dumb," Persephone protested. "I like reading the scrollazine's polls. Usually." Why was she defending that poll? she wondered. Well, she actually did think some polls and quizzes were fun to read.

"It's fluff," he huffed. "And annoying."

"Oh, poor you," she said, folding her arms. "You got labeled Most Fascinating. Who wouldn't want to be fascinating? Do you think I liked my label? Most Dependable?"

Hades sent her a confused look. "What's wrong with being dependable?

She studied his expression. Did he really not get it? Sometimes boys could be a little dense about stuff like this. She shrugged. "Never mind."

154

"Listen, I've got to help the guys with the rest of the equipment," he said abruptly.

Wait! Was he telling her to leave him alone? How had their conversation gotten so off track? Persephone wondered in alarm. They were beginning to act like Aphrodite and Ares did when they were on the verge of an argument.

She had to fix things. But before she could explain that she'd had no idea Eurydice would blab her confidences all over the universe, and before she could tell Hades she was sorry he'd been put on the spot, Apollo called to him and he turned away.

His back to Persephone, Hades paused. "That poll doesn't matter," he said. "And I don't care if the whole school thinks I'm bad news. You know the real me. That's what's important. And I know the real you. At least I thought I did before you hooked up with Eurydice."

Feeling stunned, Persephone just stood there for a minute, watching him go over to help his friends gather the band instruments together so they could carry everything back inside the Academy.

Why hadn't he given her a chance to explain? Why did he just assume she was the one who'd told Eurydice about everyone thinking he was bad news? Well, she may have said that, but he didn't know for sure. Besides, no one thought he was bad news now. That was stuff that had happened way early in the year.

She felt like crying. But she was mad now too. How *dare* Hades try to tell her that she shouldn't be friends with Eurydice. Okay, he may not have said that exactly, but he'd implied it.

What if she'd listened to her three best friends back when they'd told her *he* was bad news? She wouldn't even be friends with him right now! Didn't he get that?

Well, she wasn't going to dump Eurydice just because Hades didn't like her. She'd never dump one friend for another. No way!

Trying to ignore the tight feeling in the pit of her stomach, Persephone turned her back on him. Then she jumped down from the stage and stomped off to lunch.

10

Judging

Hades

BAD NEWS... BAD NEWS...

The words from Orpheus and Eurydice's new song echoed in Hades' head. After Persephone left the stage and stomped off, he hopped from the stage himself and went in the other direction without a word to the rest of the band. He didn't feel like being around people in the cafeteria, so instead he headed for the forest.

Orpheus had told him that Eurydice was a good influence on his music. Maybe so. But that girl was a bad influence on Persephone, in Hades' opinion.

He sighed as that familiar prickly feeling that meant there was trouble in the Underworld hit him again. What now? After summoning Midnight, he mounted the stallion and galloped below the earth.

When he touched down in the Underworld, he gazed across the river to the opposite shore. There were even more girls hanging around over there than before. "Hades! Hades! We love Hades!" they chanted together. Then they screamed and pretended to swoon.

Not wanting to encourage them, Hades tried to ignore them. Only it was kind of cute in a way—all this adoration. Still, hanging around like this was a dangerous thing for them to do!

Charon pulled up in the ferryboat. "See this?" he

asked by way of greeting. He held up a silver coin.

"It's an obol. So?" Hades asked. All the shades paid an obol to ride the ferry.

To Hades' surprise Charon put the obol between his teeth and bit down on it. It cracked in half! He handed the pieces to Hades.

"It's candy. Fake," said Charon. "They gave me fake coins!" He gestured toward two girl shades who'd just gotten off his boat. They were jumping up and down at the entrance to the Underworld, as if thrilled to be there.

Hades waved them over. "Why not just give him real obols?" he asked them. He'd never seen shades so excited and lively before. Usually they were pretty grim.

"We'd already spent our allowances," one girl told him.

"But we knew if we didn't get to meet you, we'd just absolutely *die*!" the other one added.

"That's the whole problem," charged Charon. "You can't be here. Because you *aren't* dead!"

Hades' eyes widened. "Not dead? Then how—" Just then he noticed the girls were holding copies of *Teen Scrollazine.* Did this have something to do with that poll?

"They're living mortals. Not shades. They tricked their way in," said the ferryboat captain, shaking his head in disbelief. "First time I've been fooled in an eternity."

Alarmed, Hades tried to rush the girls back on board the ferryboat for the return trip out of the Underworld. "You've got to get out of here before—"

"Too late," Charon said in his mournful voice. He looked skyward.

Hades glanced up too, knowing what he'd see. The Furies. They were back. The three women with wild hair and belts made out of live snakes were flying overhead, eyeing the mortal girls.

Waving up at them, Hades forced a grin, trying to keep things light. "Hey! Thanks for dropping by, but I've got things covered. These girls don't need to be punished. Turns out they're not shades after all. They don't belong here, so I'll just send them on home."

The Furies shook their heads, their snakes hissing.

"Negatory on the sending them home," said Alecto.

"You know the rules," said Megaera.

"Once someone's in the Underworld, they're in," said Tisiphone.

"For all eternity," the flying Furies chorused together.

The two mortal trespassers clung to each other, their faces scared now.

"Aw, they didn't know what would happen. Let them go," Hades told the Furies, trying to sound calm and reasonable. "That way they can warn their other mortal friends to stay away from the Underworld until they're actually dead."

"Right, girls?" He eyed the trespassers, who nodded quickly.

The Furies didn't want to let the girls go, but eventually their sense of fairness made them agree.

"All right," said Tisiphone. "They can leave."

"On one condition," added Alecto.

"That we get first crack at deciding on punishments for any other trespassers in the future," said Megaera.

Hades nodded. "Deal!" Since the Furies always added a condition to any pact they made, he'd been expecting something like this.

Now that the two girls had been set free, Charon ferried them back to safety. Meanwhile, Hades flew to the the far bank of the River Styx and got busy posting signs to keep other trespassers away. His signs said things like: IF YOU'RE NOT A SHADE—SHOO! KEEP OUT, UNLESS YOU'RE DEAD! DO NOT ENTER BECAUSE YOU WILL NEVER GET OUT!

He staked all the signs in the ground and then stood back to survey them. "That should keep anyone else from trying to sneak in," he said to Midnight. "I hope."

Even after his work was done, he really didn't feel like returning to the Academy. Classes were almost over for the day anyway. So instead he mounted Midnight and escaped deeper into the Underworld. He went all the way to the brink of Tartarus, where he could be alone. Just him, the rivers of lava, and his gloomy thoughts about what had happened with Persephone.

11

Free Spirits

Persephone

PERSEPHONE SAT ON THE SPARE BED IN ARTEMIS'S dorm room after school on Friday and plucked the strings on the lyre she was holding.

Owooo! Artemis's three hounds howled. Over at her desk Artemis looked up from the arrow tips she was filing, and winced.

It wasn't the dogs' howling that was making her

cringe, Persephone knew. It was the sour notes coming from the lyre she held in her hands. With Eurydice's encouragement, she had taken up the instrument on Wednesday. Now it was Friday, and in her own opinion she'd only gotten worse. Even though she'd been practicing every spare minute—for over two whole days!

A quick knock sounded at the door, and Athena peeked inside. Her eyes went to Persephone. "Did you switch to a Music-ology class when I wasn't looking?"

Persephone grinned at Athena and set the lyre she'd been playing—well, *attempting* to play—back in its case on the end of the bed. "So, what do you think of my chances as a future rock star?" she asked teasingly.

"Um," Athena hedged.

"Well," Artemis mumbled.

"Just kidding. I know I'm bad," Persephone admitted. "I'm all green thumbs. Good at gardening. Not at music!"

"Well, we can't be good at everything, I guess," said Athena.

Artemis nodded. "Yeah, I can sing a little, but I'm not nearly as musical as Apollo. He got most of the family talent in that area. He's naturally gifted."

"On the other hand he and his band members spend hours practicing, right?" Athena noted. She glanced at Persephone. "Are you willing to practice as long and hard as they do to become good on an instrument?"

"We kind of hope not," Artemis joked, before Persephone could answer. "I'm not sure my dogs' ears can take it if you keep practicing."

Persephone giggled. "Don't worry. I just wanted to try something new is all. Break out of my *dependable* box." Also, she'd been trying to take her mind off Hades. The two of them hadn't talked since the concert last Tuesday.

"Are you still thinking about that *Teen Scrollazine*

poll?" Athena asked in surprise. She came in and sat down on one of Artemis's desk chairs. "I'd forgotten all about it."

"She's not the only one obsessing over it. Ares' and Apollo's egos have swollen to twice normal size ever since they were voted Handsomest and Best Musician," complained Artemis.

"Being voted Strongest has gone to Heracles' head too," said Athena. "He keeps walking around flexing his muscles. What about Hades?"

The two girls looked at Persephone.

"I don't know," she admitted. "We haven't talked at all in the last few days. Hades told me he doesn't like how I've been acting since Eurydice and Orpheus came."

Athena's and Artemis's expressions became concerned.

"Maybe he's jealous or something. Maybe he thinks

you have a crush on Orpheus," Artemis suggested.

"Who doesn't?" said Persephone, eyeing the Orpheus poster hanging on Artemis's wall. Then she flopped over to lie on her side. Propping herself up on one elbow, she gazed at her friends. "It's not a real crush, though. It's only for fun. Like crushing on a hero you read about in a bookscroll. Know what I mean?"

"Of course," Athena said.

Artemis nodded.

"Besides, that's not the problem," Persephone went on. "Hades isn't jealous or anything. He just thinks maybe Eurydice is a bad influence, and so he—"

Suddenly the door burst open, and Aphrodite came in without even knocking. She shot Persephone a worried glance. "Have you seen our kitten?"

Persephone sat up. "Adonis? No. He's not in your room?"

She'd brought Adonis here to the dorm when she'd decided to stay with Artemis the rest of the week. By now, he got along fine with Artemis's rambunctious dogs, but the idea of leaving the four pets unsupervised in this room together while the girls were in class had made Persephone a little nervous. So she'd left the kitten in Aphrodite's care instead.

"I checked just now," said Aphrodite. "He's not there. Eurydice was supposed to go by to feed and play with him while I was gone, then come and meet me at the Supernatural Market for nectar shakes. But she never showed up. The rest of you were invited too. She didn't tell you?"

"I haven't seen her all day," said Persephone, growing worried. Eurydice had better be taking good care of Adonis—wherever she'd gone off to with him. And she should've asked permission before taking him anywhere!

"I haven't seen her either," said Athena.

"I did," Artemis told them. "About an hour or so ago. She was walking down the hall with somebody. Their backs were to me, though, and I wasn't paying all that much attention, so I'm not sure who she was with."

Aphrodite went over to the window and scanned the courtyard below. "I don't see her anywhere." She turned her head toward Artemis. "She only stayed with me Tuesday night, then spent Wednesday with Iris and Thursday with Atë. Was she with one of them maybe?"

This was all news to Persephone. Lots of girls from the dorm had been hanging out in Aphrodite's room after class this week having fun till bedtime, including Eurydice. She'd thought the girl had slept over there the last three nights as planned.

She'd simply assumed that Eurydice preferred Aphrodite's company to hers. But apparently that pink-haired girl was even more fickle than Persephone had realized! Being a free spirit was one thing, but hurting people's feelings and letting them down really wasn't very nice.

"Atë! That's who it was," Artemis told Aphrodite. "I didn't see Adonis with them. But I do remember that Eurydice was carrying that woven bag of yours. The one with the ginormous flower on it."

Aphrodite turned from the window, her face even more concerned now. "That's the bag I sometimes carry Adonis in! Oh, I really don't like the idea of her taking him off somewhere. She's just not very . . . *responsible.*"

Hearing the worry in Aphrodite's voice, Persephone got even more worried. Because Aphrodite was right. Eurydice was *not* a responsible person.

"I'm sure Eurydice and Adonis are around here somewhere," Athena said reassuringly. She headed for the door. "Let's go look for them."

The four friends split up so they could cover more area and search more quickly. Athena took the classroom floors. Artemis said she'd try the gym and sports fields.

Aphrodite and Persephone began checking the rooms up and down the girls' dorm hall. As they were knocking on doors, Atë appeared in the hall.

"Thank godness I found you!" she told them breathlessly. "I flew Eurydice down to the Underworld by winged sandal and she hasn't come back out. It's been almost an hour, and I'm getting panicked."

"What? She can't go into the Underworld!" said Persephone. "She's mortal. And not dead. Why would she— Wait a minute! You didn't *dare* her to go there, did you?"

Atë looked away. "Um, maybe. We were playing with your kitten. Then we started playing Truth or Dare, and she—"

"Did she take Adonis with her?" Aphrodite demanded.

"Yeah, I guess," Atë admitted. "She said you'd told her to take care of him."

Persephone grabbed Aphrodite's arm. "She can't make her sandals fly on her own. C'mon. We have to go after her!" Together they dashed downstairs, where they kicked off their sandals so hard that the sandals hit the wall just inside MOA's front doors. *Bam! Bam! Bam! Bam!* Then the girls snatched some winged sandals from the basket and hurried outside.

As Persephone was slipping on her flying sandals, she saw that Atë had followed them. "Find Athena and Artemis and tell them Aphrodite and I have gone to the Underworld, okay?" she told the spirit-goddess.

"Okay," said Atë. She shifted from one foot to the other, clasping her hands together. "I have to tell you something else. But it wasn't my fault!"

Persephone's breath caught with fear. Suspicious, she jumped up. Her sandals hovered a few inches above the ground, their wings gently flapping as she gripped Atë's arm and studied her face. "Please tell me you didn't dare Eurydice to do something even dumber than entering the Underworld."

Behind them one of MOA's front doors had opened while she'd spoken. Orpheus had come outside and overheard. "What?" he exploded. "Eurydice is in the Underworld?"

Atë looked even more nervous now. "Well, I might've suggested or maybe even kind of dared her to dance in the Forbidden Meadow," she admitted reluctantly. "But I was *joking.* I never expected her to take the idea seriously!"

"Are you bonkers!" Orpheus yelled. "There are nests of poisonous snakes in that meadow! Hades told me so himself." His hand was white-knuckled where it clenched his lyre. It was slung low at his hip, suspended from a strap that looped around his neck.

Atë gasped and pressed her hands to her cheeks. "Oh! I—I didn't know. I'm so sorry."

"'Sorry' isn't much help now. I only hope she didn't take Adonis there too!" Aphrodite said. She was so upset, her face wore a deep frown, an expression she usually avoided for fear of wrinkles.

"Let's get moving," Persephone urged.

"Wait for me," said Orpheus. While they'd been speaking, he'd ducked inside and grabbed a pair of winged sandals too. Now he insisted on going with them.

"You can't enter the Underworld," Persephone told him. "You're mortal."

"Just let me come as far as I can," he pleaded. "I need to know Eurydice is all right the minute you have news."

Giving in, they waited for him to slip on his sandals. Atë seemed relieved that she wasn't going to have to personally deal with the trouble she'd caused. She slinked away now, leaving them to it.

Soon Orpheus stood between Aphrodite and Persephone, holding tight to their hands. The three of them zoomed from the Academy, through the forest, and down to Earth.

As they neared the River Styx, Persephone studied the warning signs posted below on the near bank of the river, opposite from the Underworld. They were new, obviously meant to keep trespassers away. Apparently Eurydice had ignored them.

To Persephone's surprise Hades was down there too, talking to some of the mortal girls who were still hanging around in spite of the signs. After gliding to a landing near him, she, Aphrodite, and Orpheus started asking anxious questions all at the same time. "Have you seen Eurydice? Or Adonis?"

When Hades shook his head, Persephone explained in as few words as possible what they feared Eurydice had done.

"Godsamighty!" he exclaimed.

"We have to find her!" said Orpheus. He looked as upset as Persephone felt.

Quickly Hades whistled for his chariot. When it arrived, Persephone and Aphrodite jumped inside with him. Orpheus tried to climb in too.

"Sorry. You can't come," said Hades, blocking his way.

"But—," blustered Orpheus.

"I know you're worried, but you have to wait here," said Persephone. "No mortals allowed, remember?"

"We'll do everything we can to help Eurydice. We promise," Aphrodite told him.

Orpheus swallowed hard. "All right," he said reluctantly. He remained on the riverbank clutching his lyre, and watched them zoom across the river.

When they reached the Underworld, their chariot flew on, passing over Cerberus and the line of shades waiting to be sorted out. Soon they were hovering above the Forbidden Meadow.

"There's Eurydice," said Persephone, pointing. The foolish girl was whirling and twirling down in the meadow as if she hadn't a care in the world. The straps of the bag she'd borrowed from Aphrodite's room hung over one of her shoulders. Adonis was cuddled in her arms!

Hades skillfully took the chariot lower, tilting it toward Eurydice when they drew near. The pink-haired girl waved, delighted to see them. She didn't seem to understand how dangerous her situation was. Aphrodite and Persephone leaned out of the chariot as far as they dared, each reaching out a hand.

"Grab on!" Persephone called out to Eurydice.

"But don't drop Adonis!" Aphrodite yelled.

At their words the grinning Eurydice nodded and set the kitten inside the woven bag.

Swoosh! The chariot zoomed past her, right overhead without making contact. She'd been so busy with the bag, she hadn't lifted her hands in time to grab on. And now their rescue attempt had stirred the snakes! As the chariot circled back again, Persephone heard a warning rattle down below.

Eurydice's head gave a jerk. "Snakes!" she screamed. Finally the girl realized what trouble she was in. Several snakes slithered close to her now, rattling their tails and hissing. *Ssss. Ssss.*

"Help!" Eurydice called. She looked up, reaching

both arms high now. The bag holding Adonis dangled from her right shoulder.

"Hurry!" Persephone urged Hades. He was already readying the chariot for another try.

Below them the rattling sound grew louder. The snakes around the frightened girl coiled, lifting their heads and baring their fangs.

Swoosh! Persephone and Aphrodite whipped their arms out as the chariot dipped at a dangerous angle toward Eurydice once again. The goddessgirls each grabbed one of Eurydice's hands in theirs.

A split second later the snakes lashed out. But they only caught air. Their pink-haired prey was gone. Rescued!

Using all their strength, Persephone and Aphrodite managed to pull Eurydice—and the bag with Adonis—safely inside the chariot. All three girls collapsed on the chariot floor and exchanged wide-eyed looks of relief.

"You okay?" Hades called back to them as he guided them away from the meadow.

"Yes," the girls replied breathlessly.

Aphrodite took the bag from Eurydice and reached inside to check on Adonis. "What about you? Are you okay, little cutie-wootie!" she asked, petting his sleek black-and-white fur.

Persephone scooted closer so she could pet him too. "We were worried about you," she cooed, cuddling his paws, which were as white as the Underworld's asphodel blossoms. Loving the attention, the kitten flopped onto its back, purring and nuzzling their fingers with its pink nose.

"Um, hello? I'm safe too, if anyone cares," said Eurydice, sounding a little annoyed at being ignored.

"How did you get into the Underworld without Charon seeing you?" Hades demanded.

Eurydice shrugged. "I used one of those potions that makes you invisible."

Her eyes shifted to Persephone. "We learned about them in your Spell-ology class, remember? I saw one on Aphrodite's shelf today when I was playing with Adonis. So when Atë dared me to come here with her, I just sort of borrowed the potion on a whim. Is she mad that I used it to slip away from her? It wore off right after I got into the Underworld. So no harm done, right?"

The other two girls and Hades all glared at her.

"No harm?" Hades echoed. "Unless we get very lucky, this is still going to be a disaster of huge magnitude."

"Oh, lighten up, gloomster," Eurydice teased. She was smiling again, not seeming to care how much trouble she'd caused or how much trouble she might still be in.

Suddenly she sat up straight, concentrating very hard on whatever she was thinking about right then. "Wait." She hummed a few notes. Then she looked around, her eyes searching the chariot.

"That rescue gave me a great song idea! I need to write down the words before I forget, so I can include the song in my next concert with Orpheus. Does anyone have any blank papyrus?"

"Hush," Hades warned her. "They'll hear you."

"Who?" asked Eurydice.

Hearing a strange cackling sound, Persephone peeked out of the chariot. The other girls did too. Glancing behind her as they flew toward the River Styx, she noticed someone—three someones, actually—chasing after the chariot. As the trio gained on them, she saw it was the three Furies!

"Duck down," Hades ordered Eurydice, but she didn't

listen. And then it was too late. The Furies spotted her.

"Who's that pink-haired girl?" one of them called out.

"Great. Just great," Persephone heard Hades mutter under his breath.

Though she'd never met the Furies, Persephone knew each of their names. Hades had told her all about them. About how powerful they were in the Underworld, and how persnickety they could be about matters of justice. Especially when it came to shades . . . or mortals who entered the Underworld without actually being dead.

All too soon the Furies pulled up alongside them. They eyed Eurydice suspiciously.

Oblivious to the trouble she was in, Eurydice smiled brightly at them. "Excuse me," she said. "Do you happen to have a sheet of papyrus you could spare?"

"Who are you?" Megaera demanded.

"Me? I'm actually pretty famous. Maybe you've heard of me—Eurydice? I could give you an autograph if you do have some papyrus I can use. Oh, and also a pen?" She raised her brows hopefully.

"Stop asking," cautioned Persephone. "You'll only make things worse."

"Worse than what?" asked Eurydice, still not getting how worried she should be.

Tisiphone looked her up and down. "She looks mortal to me, and very much alive."

"I am," Eurydice informed her before Persephone could clap a hand over the girl's mouth to stop her from speaking.

"Aha!" The three Furies each pointed an accusing bony finger at Eurydice.

She cocked her head in puzzlement. "So is that a 'no' to the papyrus?"

Just then Alecto and Megaera reached for her. Suddenly Eurydice had the sense to be scared. Her eyes went wide and she drew back. Instinctively Persephone and Aphrodite moved closer to her, even though they knew it was hopeless to try to interfere with the Furies' justice.

They were still about a quarter mile from the river by now. Tisiphone glanced at Hades for support. "Mortal trespassers must remain in the Underworld. Our deal, remember?"

Hades nodded, then tugged on the reins, slowing the chariot. "I'm sorry, Eurydice, but what she said is true." He sent the girl a grim stare. "Once you enter the Underworld, you're in forever. Which you might have known if you'd read my warning signs."

Eurydice's eyes widened. "But I heard you let two mortal trespassers in the Underworld return to Earth just the other day."

Still holding the reins in one hand, Hades ran the fingers of his other hand through his dark hair in frustration. "It took some powerful convincing to get the Furies to release them. And a promise from me to let justice be done if any other mortals tried to sneak in."

"But what about Persephone and Aphrodite? They come and go as they like," Eurydice argued.

"We're immortal," Aphrodite explained. "Mortals don't have the same privileges."

Eurydice turned pleading eyes on Persephone. "You *can't* let them keep me here. I have concert dates next week."

Persephone gazed at Hades beseechingly. "There's nothing you can do?"

"I can't break the rules of the Underworld again," he said flatly. "I promised. If I go back on my word, my authority here will be called into question. Everyone will think they can break the rules. The shades might try to sneak into the Elysian Fields. Or even out of the Underworld!"

Hades and the goddessgirls watched helplessly as the three cackling Furies plucked Eurydice from the chariot. "You're ours now, girl!" said Alecto.

But Eurydice wasn't going to go quietly. "Put me down, you dumb Furies!" she commanded, struggling in their hold. "I'm not staying here. It's way too icky."

Alecto, Tisiphone, and Megaera gasped. They weren't used to being shown such disrespect. However, the shades in the field below studied the girl in admiration. None of *them* had ever dared rebel like that.

Persephone hoped it didn't put ideas in their heads. Hades would soon have a revolt on his hands!

"The whole world will be *furious* with you if I don't show up for my concerts," Eurydice argued. "Including Principal Zeus! He loves Orpheus's and my music."

Though her words were forceful, her voice trembled. She was afraid now.

"Who's Orpheus?" asked Alecto. But at that moment the Furies lost their grip on the wiggling Eurydice.

And then, just like when she'd flown in the winged sandals for the first time, Eurydice was suddenly falling. Only, this time Persephone wasn't there to grab on to her hand and save her!

12

Rules Are Rules

Hades

HANG ON!" HADES CALLED TO PERSEPHONE and Aphrodite as he swooped their chariot around to go to Eurydice's rescue. The horses went into a steep dive and brought the chariot directly under her as she fell. *Whomp!* She dropped unharmed right into a seat. Relieved, Hades set the chariot down in a meadow of white asphodel, and everyone got out.

In the distance Charon's ferry had just arrived here at the Underworld side of the River Styx again. "If I hurry, I might have time to get on board before it leaves," Aphrodite murmured. "I'll take Adonis home, where he'll be safe, okay?" She glanced warily up at the Furies as if concerned they might suddenly decide they had the right to keep a mortal *kitten* in the Underworld too!

"Good idea," Persephone told her. She gave the kitten one last pat. Then Aphrodite was winging off for the ferry, clutching the bag that held Adonis.

Out of the blue, music began to play. Lyre music.

It was far away and faint, but still the Furies' ears perked up. "What's that sound?" asked Alecto.

"That's O! Orpheus!" Eurydice called to the Furies. "The musician I was telling you about. He's playing his lyre somewhere around here, but not too close from the sound of it." She craned her neck, trying to see where he might be.

"We left him on the far side of the river," Hades told her. Keeping an eye on the Furies, he noticed that Orpheus's music had entranced them, as it did animals, mortals, and immortals too. The Furies drifted lower and settled on the ground a few feet away to sway to the beat. Their faces softened and took on dreamy, faraway expressions.

Then, as suddenly as the music had begun, it stopped.

"Make him keep playing," Megaera begged.

"And bring him closer," pleaded Tisiphone.

"Yes!" said Alecto. "We want to hear *more*."

Suddenly Hades had a brilliantly crafty idea. "Tell you what," he offered. "If you'll agree to let Eurydice leave the Underworld, I'll bring Orpheus here to play a few songs just for you."

Eurydice gasped. "But then he'd have to stay forever. Wouldn't he?"

"I'll bring him in my chariot," Hades assured her. "As

long as we don't land, his feet won't touch the ground. Technically that means he won't *step foot* on Underworld soil."

"So that wouldn't be breaking the rules!" said Persephone, sounding delighted at his clever logic. He sent her a quick smile.

"I don't know," Alecto said doubtfully.

"But his music is so delicious," said Tisiphone. "Almost like ambrosia pudding for the ears."

"More like a nectar shake," Megaera put in.

"Just imagine," Hades told them. "Orpheus Rocks the Furies. Tonight only." He spread his hands wide and assumed an expression that invited them to envision a theater sign with those words framed by torchlights.

"Let's talk this over, ladies," Tisiphone said in an excited voice.

The Furies put their heads together. After cackling among themselves for a couple of minutes, they came to a decision.

"We have a deal!" Alecto agreed. "Bring him here. After he plays for us, we'll let Eurydice leave. Under one condition."

"And what's that?" Hades asked, hoping it wasn't going to be something impossible.

"Concert now. Condition later," Tisiphone insisted.

"Yes," he told the Furies. "We accept your bargain."

"What? But they're cheating!" said Eurydice. "They should tell us the condition now so we can weigh its fairness."

The Furies bristled. "We are always fair and just!" huffed Megaera.

Hades threw the girl a warning look.

"They always add take-it-or-leave-it conditions to

agreements," he heard Persephone tell Eurydice in a quiet voice. "There's no use arguing."

Eurydice still looked dissatisfied, but luckily she held her tongue.

"C'mon," Hades murmured to Persephone. "Let's not give them a chance to back out of the bargain."

After assuring Eurydice that they would be right back, Hades and Persephone left her behind and raced his chariot back across the River Styx. When they reached Orpheus, they explained the situation with Eurydice and the deal the Furies had agreed to.

"Of course I'll go," the rock star declared in a dramatic tone. "I must rescue my muse!"

The three of them immediately flew back to the Underworld side of the river. As soon as they were above Eurydice and the Furies, Orpheus blew his muse a kiss. "We'll have you out of here in no time," he promised.

Then he slung his golden lyre into position and started strumming it. Lifting his chin, he began to sing.

Hades kept firm hold of his stallions' reins as music floated across the meadow. Staying about twenty feet off the ground, he guided the chariot in slow circles around and around the area where the Furies and Eurydice now stood.

In the fields down below, the shades stopped their work to listen. Slowly smiles spread across their faces. The smiles were kind of ghoulish but were probably the best the glum souls could manage.

The Furies were not only smiling, however. They were dancing! At least Hades guessed that's what they were doing. It was sort of like a cross between a chicken dance and the bunny hop. They were almost as bad at dancing as Principal Zeus had been before Hera had given him lessons!

A small, pale hand found its way into his free one. Persephone's hand. He looked over at her, and they both smiled at the sight of the dancing Furies and at the craziness of this whole weird, wild experience.

After Orpheus came to the end of his third song, Hades let go of Persephone's hand and motioned for the music to stop. "It's time for you to keep your side of the bargain," he called down to the Furies.

"Yeah!" added Orpheus.

"C'mon. Just one more tune!" begged Alecto.

"Now, now," tsked Tisiphone. "That wouldn't be fair and just."

"True," agreed Megaera. "Hades promised a 'few' songs, which generally indicates three."

"Oh, very well," said Alecto. Then she called up to Hades. "Our condition for releasing the trespasser is—"

"Condition? What condition?" Orpheus asked Hades.

"You didn't tell me about that! Why can't we just—"

"They always add conditions," Hades explained once again. "And we'll make it work, whatever it is."

Meanwhile, Persephone called down to the Furies. "What's the condition?"

"The three of you must depart for Earth immediately in that chariot," said Tisiphone. "The one named Eurydice may follow you, but on foot. And you must not look back to check on her progress. For if you do, the deal's off. She'll have to stay in the Underworld forever."

All three Furies folded their arms as if to remind everyone that their offers were always take-it-or-leave-it ones.

"Done!" said Hades. "We agree."

When Orpheus started to protest again, Persephone elbowed him in warning.

"I don't trust them," he muttered quietly.

"Don't worry. They'll keep their bargain. It's their job to serve justice fairly," Hades assured him. "Now let's go before they change their minds."

With a gentle tug on the reins, he turned the chariot around and headed for the dock, which was less than a quarter mile away. There, Eurydice could catch the ferry that would take her across the River Styx and out of the Underworld. He flew slowly, so she could keep pace on foot.

Although they did not look back her way, from time to time Orpheus did call to her. "Keeping up, E?" he'd ask.

"Yes, I'm here, O," she'd answer.

With Eurydice walking, the trip seemed to take forever. But eventually Hades spotted the ferry pulling into the dock just ahead.

"Almost there, E!" Orpheus called out. A few seconds of silence passed.

"E?" he asked worriedly. When there was still no reply, Orpheus—forgetting the promise they'd made—turned around.

"Oh, no!" Persephone exclaimed.

The damage had been done, so Hades looked back now too. And he saw that Eurydice, impulsive as usual, had only stopped to pick some asphodel.

Immediately the winged Furies rushed in. As Hades, Persephone, and Orpheus watched from the chariot in dismay, the cackling women lifted Eurydice from the ground and carried her away. "The one named Eurydice must stay!" they delcared.

"O!" Eurydice called. But it was too late to help her now.

It was a sad group that returned in Hades' chariot to MOA. After sending his chariot back to the Underworld, Hades followed Persephone and Orpheus to Principal

Zeus's office to deliver the bad news about what had just taken place.

Zeus sat on his golden throne with his hands folded atop his desk while the group stood before him. As he listened to the three of them speak, there was a thoughtful expression on his face.

"So Orpheus agreed to the Furies' bargain. He promised not to look back, but he did," Hades explained calmly.

"I was worried about Eurydice," said Orpheus. "I still am. What's going to happen to her in that awful place?"

"She'll be sent to the Elysian Fields," Hades told him. "It's beautiful. The dead who go there feast, play, and sing forev—"

"Enough!" Zeus interrupted. "The matter is settled. Eurydice must stay in the Underworld."

"You have got to be kidding!" Orpheus exploded. "You aren't really going to make her stay there, are you? She's not a shade. She's a superstar!"

Hades wasn't exactly happy with Zeus's verdict either. As King of the Gods he had the power to overrule the Furies. Still, his decision was a fair one. And Zeus didn't like having his decisions questioned. As Orpheus continued to protest, Principal Zeus began to glower. His bushy eyebrows lowered over his bright blue eyes. Tiny zings of electricity snapped and crackled from his fingers and ran along his forearms.

"Come on, Orpheus," Persephone whispered, tugging at the pop star's elbow. "Arguing isn't going to help." She managed to usher him out of the office before he got himself zapped. Hades followed.

Out in the hall Hades glimpsed Pheme zooming off. Now that she had wings, that girl could really move! Had she somehow managed to eavesdrop on their talk with Zeus? She was buzzing with excitement about something. What she'd just overheard, no doubt. Which meant that soon everyone at MOA would know Eurydice was stuck in the Underworld. Great.

Orpheus flung himself onto a marble bench. "Your principal doesn't seem to understand that Eurydice is my inspiration," he said in a dramatic voice. "And my good luck charm."

Hades thought of Persephone as his good luck charm sometimes too, so he knew how Orpheus felt. Still, the situation with Eurydice was pretty hopeless. Frustrated, he rammed his hands into the pockets of his tunic.

Persephone sat beside Orpheus, trying to console him. "Your talents are within yourself," she told him. "Your music will live on even if we can't rescue Eurydice."

Orpheus leaped to his feet. "No," he announced. "I will never play music again."

"Never?" Hades echoed.

"But what about your tour?" asked Persephone.

"It's off," Orpheus said. "I can't play. Not without Eurydice." With that, he trudged down the hall and up the stairs to the boys' dorm.

Persephone and Hades gazed after him in shock.

13

Flower Power

Persephone

"YOU OKAY?" A VOICE ASKED PERSEPHONE THE next morning as she stood inside the MOA greenhouse. She turned to see Athena framed in the doorway. Aphrodite was with her. And through the glass wall of the greenhouse, she saw Artemis waiting outside with her three dogs, who were romping around the courtyard.

"We heard what happened with Eurydice and Orpheus yesterday," Athena added.

"This whole thing stinks," said Aphrodite.

"Oh! Sorry. The stink is probably skunkweed," Persephone told her. "I was just making a birthday card for Hades and had a little problem with—"

"That's right! It's Saturday—his birthday," said Athena, coming closer. "I can't believe I forgot."

"Me too. It's because of all the excitement lately," said Aphrodite as she followed Athena inside.

Persephone shrugged. "That's okay. Hades might want to keep things low-key. No one's exactly in a mood for celebration around here. Wish I could think of a way out of this whole Eurydice tangle. I can't, though."

She sighed, then held up the huge card she'd made. "I came here to make him a magical singing-flower birthday card. Only, my mind was wandering as I did the spell. And voilà . . . instead of a singing-flower card, I made a singing-skunkweed one!"

When she started to open the card, her friends drew back.

"Don't worry," she told them. "This is a different one, a new card I just finished. The skunky one is already in the trash."

She opened the card all the way. A giant flower popped up from it and started singing a bouncy tune:

> *"Happy, Happy, Happy*
> *Hades' Day to you!*
> *Happy, Happy, Happy–*
> *Hope you aren't feeling blue!"*

Persephone studied her friends' faces, a little concerned she'd gone overboard. "Too much?" she asked.

"No. It's amazing!" said Athena, laughing in delight.

"Wow! I love that flower. It's humongous," said Artemis, joining them just then. She'd left her dogs outside in the courtyard playing with Apollo.

"It's my birthday gift to Hades," Persephone explained. "I mean, not this very flower exactly. I planted a whole garden of them in the Underworld as a surprise. I'm heading over there in a few minutes to show him. Fingers crossed that my timing spell works and they actually blossom today at noon as planned. And that he likes them."

"We should do something special for him here at the Academy tonight too," said Aphrodite. "Like a party."

Persephone nodded. "That would make his birthday extra . . . " She shut the card she held and then reopened it just long enough for it to sing out one more

"Happy" to complete her sentence. Everyone laughed.

"What kind of flower is that anyway?" asked Athena, once their giggles had died away.

"It's a variation of the King Protea. But I changed it some and made it a hybrid of four seeds, so I'll have to give it a new name, I suppose." Persephone glanced at her friends. "Any ideas?"

Athena tapped her chin with two fingers, thinking. Then she said, "How about calling it the Hades Hybrid?"

Persephone shook her head. "Good idea, but maybe a smidge too scientific-sounding?"

"Maybe you could call it the Bloom of Gloom?" suggested Artemis. When the others looked at her with brows raised, she added, "Well, you're going to plant it in the Underworld, right? And it's gloomy there for sure."

"I'll keep the name in mind," Persephone said tactfully. "Thanks." She slipped the card into the envelope she'd hand-made for it. Carefully she wrote Hades' name across the front.

"How about the Best Buds Forever?" mused Aphrodite. "Or maybe not. That name reminds me a little of Eurydice."

"What do you mean?" asked Persephone. Just then a butterfly drifted over to briefly settle on the tip of the feather pen she was using, before it flew off again.

"Well," said Aphrodite. "It's just that she acted like we were going to be *best buds forever* when I was with her. But then she forgot all about me when I wasn't around."

"I know what you mean!" said Persephone. Straightening, she gestured with her pen to the butterfly that was now flitting from flower to flower in the greenhouse. "She's like that butterfly over there, always getting distracted by another flower and flying off to hang out with that new one. Then she tires of it and moves on. She's just not . . ."

"Dependable?" Athena finished for her.

Persephone aimed the feather pen at her. "Exactly!"

"And being dependable is an admirable quality, right?" asked Aphrodite.

Her friends eyed her, and she knew they were remembering the *Teen Scrollazine* poll.

"Okay, I get it," Persephone said a little sheepishly.

"Yeah, Eurydice is the one who doesn't!" said Artemis.

The one . . . The one . . . An idea slowly bloomed in Persephone's head. A huge smile flashed on her face.

"Hey! I just figured out what to do!" she announced.

Her friends gave her curious looks.

"I'll explain later," she told them. "Got to get to the Underworld pronto! Noon is just around the corner." Holding the birthday card, she rushed out the greenhouse door leaving her friends staring after her in surprise.

She raced into the Academy and grabbed two pairs of winged sandals. After putting one pair on her feet, she was off to the Underworld again. If all went well, she'd be bringing Eurydice back to MOA with her!

When she arrived on the Earth side of the River Styx, she saw that hundreds of mortals had gathered. They were carrying new signs now. And they had nothing to do with the *Teen Scrollazine* poll. In fact, some were protest signs that showed just how unpopular Hades had become. Others, though, were on his side of things.

FREE EURYDICE!

HADES STINKS!

HADES IS FAIR AND JUST!

As Persephone boarded the ferry, she could hear a pounding sound that seemed to be coming from over on the Underworld side of the river. The mist shrouding the river was too thick for her to see what was causing it, though.

About halfway into the ride the mist finally parted, and she saw who was making all the racket. Hades! He was onshore, hammering tall iron posts into the ground about six inches apart.

"What are you doing?" Persephone asked him once she'd landed.

"Building a fence," he replied without glancing at her. "To keep any more mortals from entering the Underworld without permission. Decided we need more security around here."

He sounded grumpy. Now probably wasn't the best time to wish him a happy birthday. But she was determined to cheer him up.

"You look like you could use a break. And I have a surprise for you. Come with me? Pretty please?" she told him.

"I don't really like surprises. And I want to finish this," he said stubbornly.

"C'mon. It's your birthday," she coaxed in a silly singsong voice.

He was trying not to smile, but unable to help himself, he did. "Oh, all right," he said, tossing down his hammer.

"Here." She handed him the extra pair of sandals she'd brought. Once he'd slipped them on, they skimmed deeper into the Underworld at a brisk pace.

"Where are we going exactly?" he asked as they passed a group of shades harvesting asphodel flowers.

"You'll see," she replied.

Just then a shade shouted at Hades. "Are you sending Eurydice home soon? I hope so."

"No! I don't want her to go," another replied. "She's my best friend."

"No, she isn't. She's mine!" said a third shade.

"She's a troublemaker!" said a fourth.

"She's not," said the second shade. "*You're* a trouble-maker!"

They all began throwing stalks of asphodel at one another.

"Godsamighty!" Hades muttered. "Having Eurydice here is making my job ten times harder. How can just one girl disrupt the calm like this? She won't stay in the Elysians. She keeps roaming around bugging everyone. She even bugged me until I agreed to send a farewell message to Orpheus from her by magic wind. If I could figure a way to get her out of here, believe me, I would!"

"Believe me, I believe you!" Persephone told him sincerely.

Almost against his will he grinned again, his mood

seeming to lighten just a little more. Taking her hand, he sped them up. But a few minutes later he slowed, noticing where they were headed. "Are we going to my house?"

She smiled, nodding. As soon as they arrived at his castle, they leashed the wings on their sandals. Then Persephone checked the gloomdial.

"Three minutes," she told him mysteriously.

He looked around in confusion. "Till what?"

"Till . . ." Instead of finishing, she handed him the card she'd brought. When he opened it, the flower popped out and started singing:

> *"Happy, Happy, Happy*
> *Hades' Day to you!*
> *Happy, Happy, Happy–*
> *Hope you aren't feeling blue!"*

He laughed. "Cool." But then the card got stuck in a loop and wouldn't shut or stop singing.

"Sorry about that," Persephone said. She tried to take the card back, hoping to calm it down.

But Hades held it away, laughing louder than she'd ever heard him laugh before. "Man, this thing is hilarious. Did you make it?"

"Well, yes, but it's not supposed to— Here, let me see it." She reached for the card again, and this time he handed it over. But in the transfer she accidentally dropped it. The card finally fell shut and stopped looping its song.

Still chuckling, Hades picked it up. "Guess it wanted to do an encore performance."

"Yeah," she said, shrugging. Although the card was a little embarrassing, at least it had amused him!

Glancing over her shoulder at the gloomdial,

Persephone saw that it was almost exactly noon. "And speaking of performances." She directed his attention toward the castle, crossing her fingers that her surprise would work. And then suddenly—

Whoosh! Dozens of plants with buds and leaves sprouted from the ground all along the front of his castle.

Pop! Instantly they all burst into full bloom.

Together she and Hades beheld his new colorful garden full of humongous, fragrant flowers. She'd done it! She'd brought beauty to this otherwise dark province!

"Whoa!" exclaimed Hades as he gazed at the garden. "How? What?" He looked at her. "You did this?"

She nodded. She couldn't tell from his expression whether he liked it or not. "I wanted to brighten up this place some, and I thought these prickly flowers would be just the right touch. Not too sweet. Not too stark."

Hades went closer to the castle. He studied one of the

219

twelve-inch-wide flowers. Its petals were yellow in the middle, then gradually darkened to orange and then red at the tips. Some of the other flowers in the new garden had blue petals or even pink and purple ones.

"They're well-adapted to hot climates like the Underworld and can even survive a fire," explained Persephone. "So if there's ever a fire, and I know there are fires down here sometimes, it will regenerate." Realizing she was rattling on, she made herself stop and ask, "Do you like them?"

He looked up from sniffing one of the blossoms. "I *love* them," he told her. "No one has ever given me a gift before. Except for . . ."

She blinked at him. "What?"

"Nothing." Hades looked away.

No one had ever given him a gift? In that moment Persephone's heart melted with sympathy for him. She felt even more determined to make this his best birthday ever! And she had another surprise up her sleeve that might just do it.

"What are they called?" he asked. "These flowers you made."

Persephone's eyes twinkled. "I thought you'd never ask. If it's okay with you, I'm going to name them—Eurydice."

"Huh?" His nose scrunched and his head drew back in surprise. "You want to gift me with flowers called *Eurydice?*"

Persephone smiled enthusiastically. "That's right. Before you say no, just listen. Remember how the Furies said that 'the one named Eurydice' must stay in the Underworld forever?"

He nodded, still obviously confused.

"So I was thinking that we could officially name this new species of flower Eurydice. Then, as long as one or more of these flowers stay here in the Underworld, it satisfies the Furies' condition. Because 'the one named Eurydice' will be here, right? Growing in your garden. Which means that the real mortal Eurydice can leave the Underworld. Get it?"

A slow smile crossed his face as the wisdom of her plan dawned on him. "Got it. Eurydice the flowers remain here. Eurydice the mortal gets to leave. My bargain is still kept. It's brilliant!" he declared.

"Let's go tell the Furies," she suggested.

It turned out that the three Furies were as happy as Hades was to see the troublemaking Eurydice go. So were about half of the shades when they found out. The other half all thought Eurydice was their new best friend, and when they heard the news, they became even sadder than shades usually were.

But Eurydice herself was understandably delighted.

She graciously signed a few last autographs for her new shade fans before Hades handed her the pair of winged sandals Persephone had given him. Sandals that would now carry her back to MOA.

As Eurydice strapped them on, Hades drew Persephone aside. He looked much happier now than when she'd first arrived. "I need to finish my new fence. Will you girls be okay getting back to MOA on your own?"

"Sure." Persephone nodded. "See you?"

"Count on it." Grinning, he sent her a wave. "Later."

Once Persephone unleashed the wings on her sandals, she and Eurydice took each other's hands and began the journey back to the Academy. On the way Eurydice didn't even mention being excited about seeing Orpheus again. Instead she seemed to want to focus on the subject of the Underworld. Far from wanting to forget the whole experience, she kept talking about some of the things she'd seen.

"You were so right!" she gushed. "Those Elysian Fields were fabulously beautiful. And of course the Forbidden Meadow was frightening. I didn't see Tartarus, though." She sounded disappointed.

"Well, it's pretty much just swamp, lots of big boulders, lava rivers, and sulfur smell," Persephone told her. "Why are you so interested in that stinky place? You didn't miss anything, believe me!"

Eurydice laughed. "I told you I had an idea for a song about the Underworld, right? It's actually about MOA, too." She began singing:

> *"Mount Olympus lightning*
> *Forbidden Meadows frightening . . .*
> *Oh, please, please say*
> *That you'll take me away*
> *From the Uuunderworld . . .*

Just don't look back . . .

No, don't look baaack!"

"What do you think?" she asked Persephone.

"It's fantastic!" she exclaimed. "You wrote it?"

Eurydice nodded. "The melody is O's though. And I couldn't have found the words without your help. Thank you, Persy!" She smiled, and Persephone smiled back. It was hard to stay mad at this fickle, flighty, fun girl!

After that, talk drifted to boys and school and teachers. But Persephone kept humming the new song in her head. It was amazing!

By the time they reached MOA, she felt like they were best buds again. How did this girl make her feel that way so easily? It was like instant friendship, only now she knew it was not the lasting kind.

Lots of students were milling around the courtyard

enjoying the sunny day when Persephone and Eurydice touched down. The girls spied Orpheus coming down the granite steps. His gaze was downcast, his shoulders slumped with sadness. His bodyguard Viper was right behind him, keeping an eye on things as usual.

Orpheus instantly perked up when he saw the girls land. "Eurydice! You're back?" he called to them as they stilled their sandals. "Thank the gods! Now I'll be able to make music again! C'mon. I'll go get my lyre and we can get started."

He turned on his heel and ran back up the steps toward MOA's front doors. But Eurydice didn't follow him. And his bodyguard stayed put too.

"Not so fast, O," Eurydice called out dramatically. She turned toward Viper. Smiling big, she reached out her hand, which he took in his. Then the two of them half-turned toward the students in the courtyard. "I'm leaving your band, O," Eurydice announced in a loud, clear voice. "Viper and I are starting our own band."

Everyone appeared stunned by what she'd said. Including Orpheus. "Wh-what?" he asked.

"You heard me," she said. Noticing Pheme not far away, a pleased expression crossed Eurydice's face. "And anyone who didn't hear me will hopefully get the scoop soon!"

With that, Eurydice and Viper flounced off, boarded Hermes' chariot, which happened to be sitting nearby, and headed for Earth. This time Orpheus was the one left behind.

Pheme dashed in through the Academy's bronze front doors, eager to begin spreading the shocking news of the band's breakup. Persephone gazed at Orpheus. He still stood in the same exact spot on the Academy steps as when Eurydice had told him the news. His head was bent. Was he crying?

Feeling incredibly sorry for him, Persephone took the steps up to stand beside him. Aphrodite was the goddess of love, so she'd be better at helping him get over a heartbreak. But she wasn't here right now. So it was up to Persephone to console him. She searched for comforting words.

"I know that was probably a shock, and you'll miss Eurydice," she began. "But—"

Orpheus lifted his head and tossed back his thick brown hair. He gazed at her with his world-famous turquoise eyes. "I'm heartbroken," he told her. Then a big smile broke across his face. "Isn't it awesome?"

"Huh? I thought heartbreak was a bad thing," Persephone said.

"Not when you're a songwriter," he told her enthusiastically. "Losing Eurydice *twice* is the best thing that could have happened to my music. The first time, I was just angry about losing her to the Underworld. That didn't really help my music. Who wants to hear angry songs?

"But now my head is suddenly full of songs about broken hearts and stuff," he went on. "Everyone wants to hear songs like that! I'll be more famous than ever."

Without another word he dashed into the Academy. Soon his music was floating from the windows of the boys' dorm. His beautiful voice crooned one new song of heartbreak and lost love after another. It was as if a dam had broken and a river of musical creativity was flowing out of him!

Persephone didn't get it. The breakup between Orpheus and Eurydice had happened so *fast* that her head was spinning. She couldn't quite believe that Eurydice would throw Orpheus over for Viper. Something didn't smell right. And this time it wasn't the skunkweed card she'd tossed away!

14

Surprise!

Hades

"ONE, TWO, THREE ... HIT IT!"

Hades beat on the drums with his drumsticks and tapped the cymbals, keeping time with the rest of the musicians in Heavens Above. It was Saturday night, and he and the band were performing in the MOA courtyard again. His drum set was at the rear of the stage in the shadows, where he was most comfortable.

Front and center under the stage spotlight, Orpheus was strumming his lyre and singing his heart out, playing his new songs. Now that he was feeling creative again, he'd agreed to a final farewell concert. The band had been playing for two hours, so the performance was almost over.

Later tonight Orpheus would depart MOA for good and continue his tour. He'd do okay, Hades figured. Everyone seemed to like his new heartbreak songs. Some of the girls in the audience were even crying, in a happy sort of way.

Out in the courtyard Hades glimpsed Persephone. She was sitting with Aphrodite, Athena, and Artemis on the edge of a high garden box wall, sipping nectar. Behind them were beds of flowering bushes. Beyond that stood the Academy, gleaming in the twilight.

Catching his eye, Persephone waved. He grinned and waved back.

Then he got his cue. It was time for the big special effect Orpheus had asked him for. Quickly Hades cast a simple spell:

> *"Torches of flame . . .*
>
> *Bring Orpheus fame!"*

As his words died away, the special flaring torches Hades had set in place rocketed up from the middle of the stage. They created a flash of multi-colored flames all around Orpheus.

A collective gasp rose from the students in the court-yard. They craned their necks and whispered excitedly. "What's happening?" "What's going on?" he heard them say.

The special effect was electrifying, but it wasn't dangerous. It was only a bit of harmless magic—all part of a grand finale that Orpheus had planned. Hades knew only the pyrotechnics part of the plan, however. Like everyone else, he waited to see what would happen next.

As suddenly as they'd appeared, the colorful flames disappeared. And now, instead of just Orpheus at center stage, there were three people standing there.

"It's Eurydice! She's back!" someone yelled.

Hades' jaw dropped. This was unexpected!

A wild cheer went up at the sight of both Eurydice and Orpheus onstage together again. Viper was with them, but quickly stepped to the back of the stage. He wasn't a musician at all, Hades guessed. Had Eurydice only made up that story about forming a band with him? If so, why?

Moments later Eurydice began to sing, her clear lovely voice smoothly blending with Orpheus's in a duet. It was a song about the Underworld!

"Mount Olympus lightning

Forbidden Meadows frightening . . ."

The two rock stars held everyone transfixed with the beauty and power of their voices. Even Hades fell under their spell. When the last words of the song died away, there was a small silence.

Then everyone began whooping and cheering like crazy. He jerked to attention, remembering this was his cue for a final special effect. Using magic, he made the torches reappear. This time the simulated flames rose higher and brighter than ever.

They fizzed and sparked wildly for about a minute. And once they died away, Orpheus, Eurydice, and Viper were gone!

The crowd jumped to their feet, whistling and clapping. Deciding that the band's work was pretty much done, Hades hopped off the back of the stage and headed around toward Persephone and her friends. By the time he got there, the applause and cheers were dying down. Everyone was still buzzing about the performance.

"How did they both know the words?" he heard someone wonder.

"Orpheus didn't seem surprised about Eurydice's and Viper's return," someone else said.

Just as Hades reached Persephone, she braced herself with both hands to push down from the wall. Only, her hand slipped and she started to tumble. In the nick of time he put his hands on either side of her waist and safely set her on the ground.

"Whoa! Thanks," she said. She squinted up at him for a few seconds, a thoughtful look on her face. Then her eyes widened. "You're the one who rescued me at the

Orpheus Rocks the Gods concert," she said in surprise. "I just realized it."

He stuck both hands into his pockets. "No big deal."

"It was a big deal," said Aphrodite, hopping down from the wall on her own.

Persephone's other two friends jumped down too, and all four girls gazed at him in admiration.

"Yeah, she could've been crushed in that mob," Athena told him.

"Face it, god-dude, you're a hero," said Artemis. "Even if we didn't realize it till now."

Aphrodite's blue eyes sparkled more brightly. "And a hero deserves something special on his birthday. Ta-da!"

The girls all threw their arms wide and looked upward expectantly. Hades followed their gazes. Suddenly balloons magically began to fall from the sky like giant colorful raindrops. They landed all around Hades, bouncing a few times before settling down. Behind him the band launched into a rowdy version of the "Happy Birthday" song.

Eros and some of the other godboys wheeled out a cart with an enormous cake on it. Looking closer, Hades saw that a frosting map of the Underworld decorated its top.

"Happy Hades' Day!" everyone shouted.

Feeling a little dazed, Hades blew out the candles on his cake. As Persephone and her friends began handing out pieces, everyone crowded around him, teasing him about getting old, and making silly birthday jokes.

"So, I wonder what the scoop is on Eurydice and Orpheus?" Persephone asked a little later as a bunch of students sat surrounded by the balloons, eating cake in the courtyard.

Hades suspected she'd asked the question just to get

everyone to focus on something besides him. She knew he was uncomfortable with too much attention. The fact that she knew that about him, and didn't mind, was just one of the many things he liked about her.

"I know!" Apollo announced in response to what Persephone had wondered. "Just before the concert Dionysus and I caught Orpheus, Eurydice, and Viper making plans backstage. We were sworn to secrecy, though."

"But now we can reveal the truth," said Dionysus. "That they never broke up at all. It was just a publicity stunt. Apparently Eurydice sent a message from the Underworld to Orpheus outlining the whole plan, just in case she did manage to escape."

I sent message for her, Hades realized, though he hadn't known what she'd written.

"And I helped spread the word about the breakup," a voice piped up. Pheme had arrived out of nowhere as usual. "Their tour will get extra attention now. That new duet of theirs is going to be an instant megahit!"

As more students came over, the group around the cake cart grew. Hades and Persephone wound up standing a little off to the side.

"So you knew it was a publicity stunt too?" she asked him.

Hades shook his head. "Not at all. Like Apollo said, he and Dionysus—and Pheme, too, I guess—were sworn to secrecy. Orpheus and Eurydice must've figured that the fewer people who knew, the better." He grinned. "Can't say I'm not glad those two are heading back to Earth, though. Now they'll be someone else's problem."

Persephone giggled.

A small silence fell between them. He ran his fingers through his dark hair and shifted from one foot to the other.

"What?" she asked him. She must've sensed he had something more to tell her. Another thing he liked about her. She could read him like a textscroll.

"There's something I— I mean I just wanted to say, um—" Leaning down, he gave her a quick kiss on the cheek. She caught her breath. He drew back to look at her. Was she mad that he'd kissed her?

"Thank you," she said, blushing. Then her green eyes widened and she looked embarrassed. Probably for having thanked him for a kiss!

He grinned. "No. Thank *you*. For the best birthday ever." Then he added, "Remember how I said no one had ever given me a gift before?"

Persephone nodded, her eyes glistening.

"That wasn't exactly true."

She tilted her head with curiosity, watching him pull at the chain he wore around his neck. He fished it out of his tunic and showed her the amulet that hung on the end of the chain. She cupped it in her palm, studying it.

"A pomegranate seed?" she asked.

"Not just any pomegranate seed," he told her. "It's from our spitting contest. The first time we talked in the cemetery. Remember?"

"You kept one of the seeds?"

"Um, yeah." Did she think that was dorky? He couldn't tell.

"And you've worn it all this time?"

"Well, yeah." Did she think he was dumb for doing that?

"That is so . . . mega-awesome!" she exclaimed.

She smiled up at him. And it was like the sun had come out again to brighten the twilight. In his opinion this birthday was now officially the most perfect ever!

15

Don't Look Back

Persephone

IT WAS MONDAY TWO WEEKS LATER, AND PERSE-phone was skipping and twirling her way down the girls' dorm hall. She knocked on Athena's door, then Artemis's, and then Aphrodite's. When they popped out of their rooms, she held up a scroll and read it aloud:

"Dear Persephone,

We are pleased to notify you

that your Eurydice blossom has

been accepted into the Anthestiria

Flower Festival. Few are chosen for

this honor. Congratulations!

Please enter a flower-themed float

into the parade, prepare a speech,

and plan to arrive in Cyprus two

weeks from today.

Sincerely,

The Festival Acceptance

Committee"

"I've been accepted into the Anthestiria Flower Festival!" she shouted just in case her friends hadn't fully understood what the letter was all about. But they had, because they were all grinning from ear to ear. As the other three girls came out into the hall, Persephone did another little twirl, too excited to stand still.

"Awesome!" said Athena, hugging her as soon as she stopped twirling. "You worked hard for this honor!"

"Congratulations!" said Aphrodite, joining in on the hug.

"Your flower was amazing. I'm not surprised they liked it," said Artemis. She hugged Persephone too.

"Thanks!" said Persephone. "I'm a little worried about the speech part," she admitted as they drew back. "I mean, as fun as it was being onstage at Orpheus's concert that one night, the attention was mostly on Orpheus and Eurydice. During my speech all eyes will be on me." She made a *Yikes* face.

"After you write it, I'll help you edit it if you want," Athena offered.

"And Artemis and I will be your audience while you practice it. We can give you some pointers," said Aphrodite. "It'll be like a trial run."

"You guys are the best! I'd really appreciate the help," Persephone told them. "The *truth* is that without it I might not *dare* to do the speech at all!"

Her friends laughed, getting her jokey reference to the Truth or Dare game that had been the beginning of so much excitement a few weeks ago.

Aphrodite smiled at her. "Don't worry. We're all behind you on this."

"Whatever you need, we're there for you," said Athena.

"Yeah," said Artemis. "We've got your back."

Which basically meant that she could depend on them, Persephone knew. Her friends had never let her down. Dependability was just as much a part of their character as it was hers! And it was a part of Hades' character too. That's why he was so conscientious about his work in the Underworld.

As much as she'd enjoyed Eurydice's spontaneity and unpredictability, she knew *she* couldn't live that way. It would drive her crazy! And so would having undependable best friends.

So if she valued that trait in her friends, she should value it in herself, right? When she got home today, she decided, she would post that *Teen Scrollazine* poll smack dab in the middle of her bulletin board. Being dependable was something to be *proud* of!

Of course, that didn't mean she couldn't be just a little bit daring from time to time too.

"I'm going to head down to the Underworld to gather some flowers," she told her friends. "Think

Hades will help me build a float if I ask him?"

"I think you can *depend* on it!" said Athena.

Smiling, Persephone dashed down the hall. She couldn't wait to find Hades and tell him her good news! And as for that speech she'd have to give, well, it would be worth a bit of stage fright to accept the honor that was hers.

As she headed downstairs, she imagined the scene at the festival. When her name was called to speak, she would definitely *dare* to climb up onto that stage. She would get up there and give her speech.

There would be an audience, of course. And the festival committee would be sitting in a row of chairs behind her onstage, gazing on as they listened. Lucky for her, the Furies wouldn't be sitting with them, waiting to pounce on her if she made a mistake.

She grinned, thinking to herself that, just in case they did decide to show up, *she would not look back!*

247